FROM THE
NANCY DREW FILES

THE CASE: Ned asks the beautiful new girl in town to marry him. After going out with Nancy for so long, why is he engaged to someone else?

THE CONTACT: Anyone who knew Jessica Thorne before she came to River Heights. Nancy has to start looking—fast.

THE SUSPECT: Jessica Thorne, Ned's fiancée. No one knows anything about her—except that she lives alone in a luxury hotel and has loads of charm and money.

COMPLICATIONS: Jessica seems to be truly in love with Ned. She won't even accept his expensive gifts. Could she really have some other scheme in mind?

Books in The Nancy Drew Files® Series

Available from ARCHWAY Paperbacks

THE NANCY DREW FILES™ CASE · 24

TILL DEATH DO US PART

Carolyn Keene

AN ARCHWAY PAPERBACK
Published by POCKET BOOKS

New York   London   Toronto   Sydney   Tokyo   Singapore

AN ARCHWAY PAPERBACK *Original*

An Archway Paperback published by
POCKET BOOKS, a division of Simon & Schuster Inc.
1230 Avenue of the Americas, New York, NY 10020

ISBN: 0-671-68378-0

First Archway Paperback printing June 1988

10 9 8 7 6 5 4

TILL DEATH DO US PART

Chapter

One

NANCY DREW RAISED an elegant dress over her head and let it fall down around her slender figure. A sheath of turquoise silk, it left her back bare and stopped just above her knees.

Smoothing it down, she turned from her mirror with a puzzled smile. "Something's up, I know it. I just wish I could figure out what!"

Nancy's friend George Fayne was sitting cross-legged on Nancy's bed, flipping through a magazine. Trim, toned, and tan, she was a superb amateur athlete. Nearby, George's blond and

1

curvy cousin Bess Marvin was sprawled in a chair, looking exhausted. The two had stopped to visit Nancy after a late-afternoon tennis game.

Nancy didn't need to ask who had won.

"Come on, Nancy, why do you have to turn everything into a mystery?" Bess complained, fanning herself with her hand. "I mean, you're only going out with Ned, right?"

"But he's being so mysterious. First he insists that I get all dressed up, and then he refuses to tell me where we're going."

"So? Relax and enjoy yourself," George advised.

"Yeah, let him surprise you," Bess agreed.

"I wish I could. I'm trying. But it goes against my nature."

"Ned" was Ned Nickerson, Nancy's boyfriend. Normally he was the most straightforward guy in the world, but for the past three weeks—in fact, since their first, and only, date of the summer so far—he had been acting very cagey. He had been avoiding going out with her, and now, for some reason, he was turning their second date into a puzzle.

Why?

Guiltily, Nancy wondered if it could still have anything to do with the stupid disagreement they had had on their last date. Ned had claimed that he could be as good a detective as she—maybe better. Her pride hurt, she had fired back a stinging reply.

But it couldn't be that, she reasoned further. She had apologized, and that had been the end of it. Ned never held a grudge. Still, if that wasn't the reason, then what was? Crack detective that she was, Nancy had to keep trying until she figured it out.

"So, Nan, do you have a theory about what's going on?" George asked.

Nancy shook her head.

"Well, he's obviously taking you someplace fancy," Bess observed.

"Maybe Paris," George chimed in.

Nancy laughed. "Oh, right. Seriously, I wish I could guess what's going on. The suspense is driving me crazy."

Crossing to her dresser, Nancy brushed back her reddish gold hair and fixed it in place with a pair of barrettes. Next, she clipped on two silver earrings and stepped into a pair of high-heeled pumps. A dab of perfume on her throat and wrists, and she was finally ready.

Twirling around, she asked, "Okay, how do I look?"

"Hot!" Bess pronounced.

"Definitely," George agreed. "Ned isn't going to know what hit him."

"Good."

Just then there was a tap at Nancy's door. "Nancy?" It was the voice of Hannah Gruen, the Drews' longtime housekeeper. "Ned's downstairs."

"Thanks, Hannah. I'll be there in a sec," Nancy said. Grabbing her evening bag, she smiled at her friends. "Well, time's up. I guess this is one mystery I won't get to solve. Still, there's one consolation."

"What's that?" George asked.

"I'm going to knock his socks off. Are you coming down to witness it?"

"Sure, if you want us!" Bess said, standing up.

"Bess, let's wait here until they're gone," George said quietly to her cousin. "Nancy can give us the details tomorrow."

"Okay, you two," Nancy said, smiling. "And thanks."

As she descended the stairs, Nancy decided that being kept in suspense really wasn't so bad after all. It added drama to the evening—made her pulse race a bit.

Her pulse rate jumped even more when she caught sight of Ned. Tall, dark, and square-jawed, her boyfriend was always handsome. That night, though, in his dark gray suit, crisp white shirt, and maroon tie, he looked sensational. He was holding a long white box in his hands.

"Is this dressed up enough for you?" Nancy asked, pausing at the bottom of the stairs.

Ned grinned. "You look great. Here—these are for you."

Nancy took the box, opened it, and pulled back the tissue paper inside. "Oh, Ned—long-stemmed roses! They're gorgeous! It'll take a pretty big vase to hold these."

"Don't you worry about the vase," said Hannah, who had appeared unobtrusively behind them. "I'll take care of that. You two run along and have a lovely time."

"Thanks, Hannah," Nancy said, handing the box to the housekeeper. Turning to Ned, she took his arm and demanded, "So, are you finally going to tell what this is all about?"

Ned chuckled. "Nope. I'm going to keep you guessing—and don't complain. It won't do any good," he ordered, leading her out the door.

"Why do I put up with you?" Nancy said and rolled her eyes.

Ned didn't answer. Instead, he pulled open the passenger door of his car with an enigmatic smile.

Three hours later Nancy popped the last bite of her crepes suzette into her mouth, leaned back, and sighed. It was easy to see why people called Chez Louis the best restaurant in River Heights. The food was fantastic.

The view was fantastic too. She and Ned were seated at a window table that overlooked the Muskoka River. On the water a barge was pushing slowly downstream, leaving a lazy V-shaped wake behind it. To the west the sun was low, ready for a spectacular sunset.

Reaching across the table, Nancy caught Ned's hand in hers and squeezed it. "This has been great. Thank you."

"You're welcome." Ned squeezed her hand back, gazing into her eyes with a look that made Nancy melt a little inside.

She smiled weakly. Ned really is the greatest, she thought. His "surprise" had turned out to be every bit as wonderful as she had hoped. But deep inside she couldn't shake the feeling that he was up to something.

"A penny for your thoughts?" Ned asked.

Nancy grinned. "I was just wondering if you've got something else planned for tonight."

"What makes you think that?"

"Well, for one thing it's still light outside," Nancy observed. "The evening's got a lot left to go. For another, you're smiling very suspiciously."

"Me?"

"Yes, you. Come on, Ned, out with it. There's a reason for all this, isn't there?"

"All what?" he asked innocently.

"You know! The roses. This restaurant."

Ned folded his arms. "You're too curious for your own good. You know that, don't you?"

"I am not."

"Yes, you are. Tell me something, Nan, do you ever wonder what your life would be like if there were no mysteries to solve?"

Nancy laughed. "Ned, that's impossible. There will always be mysteries to solve. Anyway, why do you ask? Are you still angry about that argument we had?"

"About my detective abilities? Nope. Not after —that is, not anymore," he said with a sly smile. "Anyway, I really am curious. What *would* you do if you weren't a detective?"

"You mean if I retired?" she asked. "I think it's early for that. I'm only eighteen. I'm barely getting started."

She was avoiding his question, and Ned knew it. "Seriously, Nancy, don't you ever imagine yourself doing something else?"

"Not really," she said with a shrug. "I enjoy solving mysteries. It makes me feel—I don't know, special. Needed."

"You're very special just the way you are."

Nancy blushed happily. "Thanks." She paused. "Ned, why are you asking me this stuff?"

For the second time that evening, Ned didn't answer. Instead, he signaled the waiter for their check. When he had paid, they rose and went outside.

"What now?" Nancy asked.

"How about a walk along the river?" Ned suggested.

"Sounds wonderful."

Hand in hand, they strolled along the bank of the Muskoka. The concrete path was lined with trees and empty benches. That night they had the riverbank to themselves.

Stopping, they watched as the sun slipped below the horizon in a fiery blaze. Streaks of orange and red shot across the sky. Nancy's heart hammered as Ned's arms slipped around her. She melted against him as he kissed her.

The sky was fading from crimson to purple when Nancy finally pulled away. "Wow," she whispered. "You really know how to treat a girl."

"It's easy when she's Nancy Drew," Ned said lightly.

"Oh, you!" She hugged him hard. Then all at once a thought crossed her mind—there *was* a mystery to solve. . . .

"Nancy? What is it?" Ned asked, searching her eyes.

"Nothing important. I was just wondering —well, if maybe you're going to tell me something."

"Like what?"

"Oh, I don't know. That you're going to spend the rest of the summer in Europe, maybe. Or you're going back to Hong Kong next year. It's *something* bad, isn't it?"

"No, nothing bad."

"Then I was right!" she cried triumphantly. "The flowers—the fancy dinner—you are softening me up. You've got something up your sleeve!"

"No, nothing up my sleeve," Ned answered. "Something in my heart. Something I want to ask you."

"What?"

Releasing her, Ned reached down and took both her hands in his. Gazing into her eyes, he asked, "Nancy, will you marry me?"

Chapter

Two

NANCY WAS THUNDERSTRUCK. "N-Ned—did I hear you right?"

Ned smiled. "I hope so. I said, 'Will you marry me?'"

Nancy swallowed. She didn't know what to say. Part of her was ecstatic. Ned had just paid her a huge compliment. But another part of her was troubled. While she had never imagined marrying anyone other than Ned, she had never imagined herself married at the age of eighteen!

"Ned, I—I don't understand. This is so sudden," she said, stalling.

"Is it?" Ned asked. "We've been in love for ages now."

"True. I guess what I mean is that it's a surprise. You never mentioned wanting to get married before."

"No, but I've been thinking about it. Haven't you?"

Nancy felt her cheeks grow warm. The truth was, she hadn't.

"It makes sense to me for us to get married, Nancy," Ned said earnestly. "We're a great team. I mean, sometimes we can almost read each other's minds."

Sometimes. Right now, though, his was a puzzle to Nancy. What had brought this proposal on? How long had he been thinking about it?

"Ned, I'm not sure it does make sense. Not right now, anyway," she said. "For one thing, where would we live? You haven't graduated from college yet."

"There's housing for married students on campus," he pointed out.

"But what about money? What would we live on?"

"My savings," he said, shrugging. "Look, we can work that stuff out. What do you say, Nancy? Will you marry me?"

Turning, Nancy drifted to the railing that paralleled the walk. Below her, the surface of the river had turned murky in the twilight. What should she tell him? she wondered. She didn't want to hurt his feelings. At the same time, she didn't want to commit herself. Marriage was so final—and so grown up!

Ned joined her at the railing. Leaning on her elbows, Nancy glanced sideways. "Ned, I'm not sure what to say. Can I have a few years to think it over?"

Ned's features clouded. "This isn't a joke, Nancy."

"I know, I know. It's just that—oh, I guess there's no other way to say it. I can't marry you, Ned. Not yet."

"Okay," he said rather quickly.

"I mean, it's not as if I don't want to. Someday I will. Probably. But right now it's too soon."

"I understand."

"Look, I guess you're furious at me—"

"I'm not."

"But you've got to see it from my point of view."

"I do."

"Ned, I'm still young. There are lots of things I want to do before I— Wait a minute. What did you say?"

"I said I understand."

"You're not mad?"

Ned shrugged. "No. Should I be?"

"Well, sure," Nancy said with a frown. "I turned you down, didn't I?"

"Not really. All you said was that this isn't the right time."

"Yes, I guess I did."

She was relieved. And surprised. She had been sure he would be hurt by her rejection. But he wasn't—apparently. In fact, Ned was being very sweet.

Affection flooded through her. No wonder she loved him so much! At the same time, though, she felt a little guilty. She hated to disappoint him.

"Ned, thank you for being so understanding," she said warmly.

"No problem," he replied with a smile.

"I mean, I hardly deserve this. Not only do I get a proposal, but I get a really wonderful reaction to my no too!"

"Well, why not? It's your decision."

"I know that. I'm just glad you understand." Nancy felt reassured—and even more guilty than before. Throwing her arms around him, she added, "You are the greatest, Ned Nickerson, do you know that?"

"Well, I've had my suspicions."

"Oh, you!" She kissed him hard. "What would I do without you?"

"Beats me."

A minute later, as they strolled toward the parking lot, Nancy slipped her arm around Ned's waist. She felt terrific. Her boyfriend was the most wonderful guy on earth.

Yet for some reason her twinge of guilt wouldn't go away. It was dumb, of course. There was no need to feel bad, she knew. Yet she did. And was he really taking it as well as he said? He couldn't be. She decided to probe his feelings a bit more when they got to his car.

"Ned, are you absolutely sure you're not angry at me?" she asked, as he politely held open the passenger door. She ignored it and turned to confront him.

"Of course I'm not angry," he said.

"You're not even a little disappointed?"

"Maybe a *little*."

"Well, you don't sound it. You sound almost relieved."

"Ye—uh—I do?"

It was only a tiny slip. It probably meant nothing, Nancy decided, but she couldn't let it pass. She wanted all of their feelings to be out in the open. It was the only way to make sure that everything was truly okay.

"Ned, why did you hesitate just then? Are you saying you *are* relieved?"

"Uh—no, I'm not saying that. Don't put words in my mouth," he said sharply.

Nancy was taken aback. "What's wrong? All I asked was why you hesitated!"

"No reason."

"Ned! You're not being honest. I know you! Tell me—why did you really propose to me tonight?"

"Because I want to marry you, obviously."

"But if that's true, then why are you glad that I said no?"

"I'm not glad!"

"Yes, you are! You sound like it anyway."

Ned folded his arms. "Look, Nancy, who said I have to be miserable? I took a chance and it didn't work out, that's all. I'm not going to cry about it."

"Well—I guess I can understand that," she said uncertainly. His words made sense, yet somehow they hurt.

"I'm glad you understand. Anyway, that proposal was serious. I mean, I wouldn't ask just anyone to marry me, right?"

"No, I don't suppose you would," she said, feeling a bit better.

"There, you see? You're worrying about nothing."

In spite of herself, Nancy smiled. "Maybe I am."

"You are, I promise."

She hugged him gently. No doubt she *was*

overreacting. Deciding to get married was a big issue. Facing it was bound to make her confused.

"I'm sorry. I apologize for being suspicious," she said. "I just wanted to make sure there were no hard feelings."

"Apology accepted. Now, shall we go home?" Ned asked.

Nancy slid into the passenger seat. Ned shut her door, got in on the driver's side, and started the engine. For a while they drove in silence. Nancy felt foolish for doubting his sincerity, but, after a few minutes, her doubts returned.

He had to be hiding something. Why else would he be taking her home now, even though it was barely nine-thirty? She had to find out.

As they turned into her driveway, she said, "Ned, let's go inside. Talk a little."

Ned brought his car to an abrupt halt. "Uh, no thanks. It's getting late."

"Ned, it's only nine-thirty!"

"Sorry. I've got to be at work early tomorrow."

He was selling insurance for the summer, Nancy knew.

"Can't you spare a few minutes?"

"Not really. It's been a long day, and—"

Suddenly she couldn't take it anymore. "Ned Nickerson, I know you're hiding something!" she blurted out.

Ned was angry. "I'm not 'hiding' anything, Nancy."

"Well, then, you're acting very weird. First you propose, then you act relieved when I turn you down. Next I try to talk to you, and—bang! You take me home."

"Nancy, you're the one who's acting a little weird. I already told you, I have to get up early. Look, I really have to go. Do you mind if I don't walk you to the door?"

Nancy glared at him. Now she was *certain* that something was wrong! No way would Ned fail to take her all the way to her door. Not unless he was in a big, fat hurry to get away!

"Ned, for the last time," she said slowly, "is there something bothering you?"

He looked down. "I already told you, no. Now good night, okay?"

Without a word, Nancy got out and slammed her door. She was starting to seethe. Ned was holding something back. She was positive.

But what? By the time she reached the top of her steps and turned to look back, his car was halfway down the street.

"Strange," George pronounced the following evening.

"Definitely bizarre," Bess agreed, shaking her head.

Nancy sighed. She, Bess, and George were eating at an Italian restaurant. All day she had been trying to figure out Ned's odd behavior, but it was no use. If he didn't really want to marry her, then he shouldn't have proposed.

"Did you try calling him at work?" George asked.

"Several times. But the secretary kept telling me he was out."

"I think there must be a logical explanation," Bess remarked.

"I hope so," Nancy said.

Twirling some more spaghetti onto her fork, Bess continued, "You know, maybe he really *was* upset when you turned him down."

"Maybe, but why didn't he just say that?" Nancy asked, feeling uneasy.

"You know how boys are—they're afraid that if they show their emotions they'll look uncool."

"Not Ned." Nancy shook her head. "He's always honest about how he feels. Or at least he was until last night."

"I wonder what he would have done if you'd said yes?" Bess mused.

Nancy had asked herself that question too —but didn't have any answer. For several minutes the three ate in silence. When the last of her pasta was gone, Nancy finished her soda and swirled the ice around with her straw.

"I don't know where to go from here," she admitted. "Should I drop it, or try to talk to him again?"

"Go swimming," Bess advised.

The three had been invited to a pool party that evening. But Nancy definitely wasn't in a party mood.

"No. I think I'd rather go home," she said.

"Don't do that. Anyway, we promised we'd be there," Bess reminded her.

"Maybe Ned will be at the party too," George hinted. "You could—talk to him."

Making up her mind, Nancy reached for the check. "I'm convinced," she said. "Let's go."

The party was in full swing when they arrived. People were splashing in the pool, talking on the lawn, and dancing on the patio. As George had guessed, Ned was there. Nancy spotted him right away. He was dancing, but it was the girl he was dancing with who riveted Nancy's attention.

She was gorgeous, a raven-haired beauty with flawless skin, a lovely face, and a figure that would have made any model envious. Who was she? Nancy wondered. She had never seen her before. She edged closer.

The girl danced up to Ned, swinging her body with practiced ease. She was wearing a tight, white-denim miniskirt and a bright red T-shirt with the sleeves rolled up. Her long, tanned legs moved gracefully in time to the music. She was smiling at Ned, Nancy saw, and Ned was smiling back.

Would Ned notice her? Nancy stood at the edge of the patio for two complete songs. Ned didn't look over in her direction once. He was totally absorbed in the dark-haired girl. She was absorbed in Ned too. If she smiled at him any harder, Nancy thought, her cheeks would crack.

Finally Nancy turned away. If that's the way Ned wanted to be, then let him! Obviously, his proposal the night before had not been serious. If it had, he wouldn't be paying so much attention to this other girl.

George joined Nancy at the refreshment table. "You saw them, huh?" she remarked. "I can tell by the look on your face."

"Who couldn't notice them?" Nancy responded, pouring herself a soda.

"Who is she?" George asked.

"I don't know—and I don't care," Nancy said, her mouth drawn in a tight line.

"Nan, if I didn't know better I'd say you're jealous."

"Me? Jealous? That's a laugh. As far as I'm concerned, Ned's free to do what he wants. We haven't made any commitments."

"Then why do you keep looking over at him?"

Nancy snapped her head around. "I wasn't looking at him."

George coughed. "Right, Nan."

Nancy's gaze drifted back to the patio. "Well, I wasn't. I was just, uh—admiring the lights along the pool."

Suddenly the music stopped. Couples began to drift away from the patio. Ned and the dark-haired girl stood close to each other for a moment, talking. Then they kissed lightly. Nancy's stomach knotted.

"Did you see that!" she gasped.

She watched as Ned and the girl parted. Ned walked over to join a group that was organizing a volleyball game, and the girl headed toward Nancy.

"Uh-oh, she's coming over here. What am I going to say, George? George?" Looking around, Nancy saw her friend had disappeared. Where had she gone? Nancy wondered.

The girl was even prettier close up than she had been from a distance. Sashaying up, she flashed Nancy a dazzling smile.

"Hi, you're Nancy Drew, aren't you? You must be, with that beautiful red hair. Everyone says you're the best detective around. Solving crimes must be exciting! Oh, but where are my manners —my name's Jessica Thorne," she said, thrusting out her hand.

Shaking hands, Nancy said, "I don't believe I've seen you around here before."

"No, I'm new to River Heights. And you know what? I love it! This is just the cutest little town I've ever seen."

Cute? Nancy felt her eyes narrow. River Heights wasn't exactly "cute." It wasn't so little anymore either.

"Where are you from?" she asked.

"Chicago."

"Are you visiting for the summer?"

"Oh, no, I'm planning to stay a *loooong* time," she said, throwing a lingering glance at Ned. "I'm living at the Royal Hotel."

Nancy's eyebrows lifted. The Royal Hotel was the nicest—and most expensive—in town. Why was Jessica living *there*?

All at once, Nancy didn't want to talk to Jessica anymore. She didn't like Jessica's condescending attitude. "Well, I hope you enjoy yourself here," she said, turning away.

"Wait! Don't go yet," Jessica pleaded, catching Nancy's arm. Nancy stopped. "I was hoping to talk to you some more. I don't know too many people here yet, and—"

"And?"

"Well, to tell you the truth, I was hoping you could tell me about Ned," she said, her expression softening.

"What do you want to know?"

"Everything! He's the greatest, don't you think? Anyway, he told me that you and he are sort of—well, buddies."

Buddies? Nancy's blood began to boil. They were a lot more than that!

"Sure, we're close," she said coolly. "In fact, we're so close that he asked me to marry him last night."

Nancy's devastating barb had no effect. Jessica merely smiled. "Really?" she remarked. "You must have dreamed it."

"No, I didn't dream it. It really happened."

"But it couldn't have," Jessica said, shaking her head with a laugh.

"Why not?"

"Because just a minute ago Ned got engaged to me!"

Chapter

Three

"YOU'RE KIDDING!"

Nancy meant her words. Jessica *had* to be pulling her leg!

Jessica was completely calm. "I'm not *kidding*. It's true. Ned and I are engaged."

"I don't believe it."

"Why would I lie?"

"I don't know, but it's impossible. Ned wouldn't do something like that—not twenty-four hours after proposing to me."

"Well, you're wrong." Jessica folded her arms. "In fact, I think *you're* the one who's lying. Ned didn't mention proposing to you. I think you made that up because you're jealous."

Nancy smiled, but her face felt slightly stiff. "Well, there's an easy way to find out the truth. . . . " She glanced meaningfully toward the volleyball game.

"You're right," Jessica agreed, following Nancy's gaze. "And that's exactly what I'm going to do—find out the truth right now!"

Whirling around, she marched straight for Ned. Nancy didn't follow. She didn't need to. She knew what Ned would say: Jessica's story was ridiculous. She was curious though. How far would the dark-haired girl carry this charade?

As she watched, Jessica walked straight into the middle of the volleyball game and grabbed Ned by the elbow. Dragging him to the sidelines, she began talking urgently. Nancy was too far away to hear what she was saying, but she had to admire Jessica's spunk. She was carrying the joke—if that's what it was—awfully far. Much farther than necessary. Nancy felt slightly uneasy.

Several minutes passed. At first Ned said nothing, but then Nancy saw him glance in her direction with a puzzled look on his face. Frowning, he asked Jessica what seemed to be a series of questions. She replied angrily, gesturing hotly in Nancy's direction. A feeling of apprehension began to steal over Nancy. If this was a joke it was awfully elaborate. And not very funny.

Then, suddenly, Ned nodded in agreement to something that Jessica was saying. Holding up his arms, he called, "Attention, everyone! Attention, please!"

All over, activity came to a halt. The volleyball game stopped. The dancing ended. When he had everyone's ear, Ned shouted, "I have an announcement to make. I'm getting married—"

A cheer went up. Smiling faces turned toward Nancy.

"—to Jessica Thorne!"

Silence. Slowly, confused faces swiveled back toward Ned—and the beaming, dark-haired girl at his side.

Nancy was in shock. She couldn't believe what was happening. It was like being trapped in a bizarre dream.

"I know a lot of you haven't met her yet, so come on over and I'll introduce you," Ned continued. "I'm sure you'll like her almost as much as I do."

At first no one moved. Then, finally, Ned's friend Dave Evans reluctantly called out, "Congratulations, Ned."

Another of his pals spoke up then too. "Yeah, best of luck, buddy."

Slowly, the partygoers shuffled up to shake Ned's hand. Few of them looked happy, however. Nancy and Ned had been together for so long! They were a River Heights legend. *What's going on?* their expressions seemed to ask.

Just then, Bess and George hurried up. "I can't believe he's doing this!" Bess said. "In public, no less!"

"Nancy, are you okay?" George asked, concerned.

Nancy looked blankly at her friend. "Where did you disappear to?"

"To get Bess."

"Oh."

Nancy barely heard anything. She was still trying to comprehend the disaster that had just befallen her. Why had Ned gotten engaged to Jessica? For revenge? To hurt her?

No. Gradually, her reason returned. Ned wouldn't do something so despicable, she knew. He wasn't that kind of guy. There had to be another explanation, she decided.

He's in love with her. A picture of him the night before—relief showing on his face— flashed through her mind. But she ignored it. She wasn't going to panic. Not yet. Not until she had all the facts. She started toward him.

The crowd parted in front of her. Silence

descended as she stopped in front of Ned and Jessica. Every ear was straining to catch her words.

She could only manage one. "Congratulations," she said, her voice sounding ten times calmer than she felt inside.

Ned regarded her without emotion. "Thanks, Nancy," he said. Then he turned to Jessica. "Would you like a soda?"

"Sure. All of a sudden I'm *very* thirsty," Jessica replied. As Ned led her away, she smiled at Nancy victoriously.

As they swept past, Nancy searched Ned's face for some clue that this was all a mistake. But there wasn't any. Ned's face was a mask. The next second Nancy spun around and dashed to her car. She knew she had to leave before she said something she might regret.

The next day was hot and humid. Nancy drove her blue Mustang with the top down, but even the breeze that whipped her hair around her head wasn't enough to cool her off.

But her mood was even hotter than the air. She was furious at Ned. Betraying her had been bad enough, but in public? That was unforgivable. There had to be an explanation. She was determined to get it.

Mapleton, where the Nickersons lived, was old and elegant. Many of the houses were stately white colonials with an occasional mock Tudor or small French chateau thrown in for variety. All the lawns were wide and sweeping, and tall trees canopied the streets.

The Nickersons' house was the nicest colonial on its block; understandable, as Mr. Nickerson's real estate business was quite successful. Nancy swung her car into the driveway, parked, and sped to the front door, timing her dash to avoid the automatic sprinkler that was throwing an arc of water back and forth across the lawn.

Mrs. Nickerson opened the front door in answer to the doorbell. She was a surprisingly tiny woman, attractive, with young-looking blue eyes, clear, unwrinkled skin, and hair that was prematurely white. She looked worried.

"Nancy! What a relief to see you. Won't you come in?"

"Thanks, Mrs. Nickerson. Is Ned here?" Nancy asked, stepping inside.

"No, he's gone to the dentist for a checkup, but please stay a minute anyway? James and I are very upset."

"I guess you heard the news?"

"Yes, Ned brought his—his fiancée"—she seemed to choke on the word—"home last night to introduce her. Needless to say, we were flabbergasted. We can't think what to do."

Mr. Nickerson was in the den. He was a tall man of around fifty with iron gray hair, keen eyes, and a firm jaw. The resemblance between him and his son was powerful. His wide mouth was usually smiling, but now it was drawn in a straight line.

"Hello, Nancy. I assume you're as devastated by the news as we are?"

"To put it mildly," Nancy said, sitting down. "Did you have any idea this was going to happen?"

"None."

"It was a complete surprise," Mrs. Nickerson agreed. "Of course, Ned has been acting strangely the last few weeks—"

"In what way?" Nancy asked.

"Well, he's been going out a lot, without saying where. He also hasn't mentioned you in conversation in ages."

"He usually does?"

"Constantly."

Ned had probably been dating Jessica for a couple of weeks, Nancy realized. That explained why he had avoided asking her out.

"Tell me," Mr. Nickerson asked, "did *you* have any inkling that this would happen?"

"No, none at all," Nancy said. She decided not

to tell them about Ned's proposal. She wanted to talk to Ned first.

"Well, I'm angry," Mr. Nickerson declared. "It was inconsiderate of Ned to spring this on us without any warning. And I'm against it. That girl isn't right for him."

"Obviously Ned thinks she is."

"That's just it," Mrs. Nickerson put in. "I'm not sure he does."

"What do you mean?"

Mrs. Nickerson thought a moment. "When Ned's around you, Nancy, he's usually relaxed. Happy. But around Jessica last night he was stiff and formal, not at all himself."

"Maybe he was just nervous. Introducing you to your future daughter-in-law, and all."

"I don't think so. I'm sure he was uncomfortable with her in general."

"Then why is he marrying her?"

"That's a good question," Mr. Nickerson replied. "Especially when he's made no secret of his intention to marry you someday."

Nancy blushed. "He's said that?"

"Many times. That's why I'm so puzzled."

So was Nancy. Ned's engagement to Jessica was making less sense all the time.

"Tell me, Mr. Nickerson, is there anything you can do to prevent the marriage?"

He shook his head. "Unfortunately, no," he

said glumly. "Both Ned and Jessica are over eighteen, which puts them above the age of consent."

"I see."

"Frankly, Edith and I have always looked forward to having you as our daughter-in-law."

"We've never mentioned it, of course," Ned's mother added hastily. "We didn't want to put pressure on you and Ned."

"Do you have any ideas?" Mr. Nickerson asked.

"I don't have a plan, if that's what you mean," Nancy said. "But I do want to talk to Ned. Who is his dentist?"

"It's Dr. Morris," Mrs. Nickerson said. She gave Nancy the address.

"Thanks. I'll catch up with him there." She rose to go. "Oh, one more thing. What was your impression of Jessica?"

The Nickersons exchanged uneasy glances. "She's pretty, of course," Mr. Nickerson said. "She's also very charming."

Mrs. Nickerson agreed. "I hate to say it, but I couldn't find anything wrong with her. She's polite, well-bred, intelligent, funny, and crazy about Ned."

"But she's not you," Mr. Nickerson added quickly.

"Thanks," Nancy said, smiling sadly. "I wish Ned felt that way."

Ten minutes later Nancy swung her Mustang into a parking lot next to the large Victorian house that had been converted into offices.

Nancy locked her car, checked the directory by the front door, and went inside. Dr. Morris's office was on the second floor. Cool, conditioned air and the antiseptic smell of a medical office hit her as she opened its door.

Ned was sitting on a couch in the waiting room. She felt a tiny stab of pain as she strode over and sat down next to him.

"Ned, we've got to talk," she said. "What's happening?"

"Oh, boy—"

"Ned, I'm not leaving until I've heard it all."

"I—"

"If you're hoping they'll call you in for your cleaning, forget it. I'll be here when you're done."

"It's not that," he said. "There's plenty of time because they can't find my records. I just don't know where to start!"

"Okay, then, how about a question to get you going?"

He nodded.

Nancy took a deep breath. Might as well start off with the biggie, she thought. "Do you love her?" she asked.

A look of horror crossed Ned's face. "*Love* her! No way! Nancy, Jessica is a cold, calculating opportunist. That's the reason I asked her to marry me!"

Chapter

Four

NANCY'S TEMPLES BEGAN to throb. Rubbing them, she said, "I don't get it. Are you saying she's blackmailing you?"

"Maybe I'd better start from the beginning."

"Please do!"

Leaning back, Ned began to talk. It had all begun the day he came home from college for the summer, he explained. He was jogging near his house when suddenly he noticed a girl—also in jogging clothes—standing at a corner with a puzzled look on her face. She was very beautiful.

"Excuse me, I'm lost," she said. "Can you tell me how to get back to the Royal Hotel?"

It was Jessica. Ned explained that she had run quite far from downtown River Heights, and offered to drive her back.

Jessica quickly—and expertly—got Ned involved with her. She was visiting River Heights, she began in the car, and she had a small toothache. Could he recommend a dentist? Ned did: Dr. Morris. Thanking him, she asked if he could also suggest a nice restaurant. Ned told her about The Greenery. It sounded fabulous, she said, but she *hated* to eat alone. Could he possibly . . . ?

So they had dinner together. And he agreed to play tennis at the country club the next day. Jessica constantly invented new excuses to keep seeing him. She played on his sympathy, building in him a sense of obligation. Ned was too polite to refuse her, and before he knew it he was spending all his free time with Jessica.

Then, slowly, she began to drop little hints into their conversations. They were innocent ones at first: "Isn't it nice that we have so much fun together, Ned?" That kind of thing. Gradually, though, the hints got heavier. "Wouldn't it be great if we got close—I mean, really *close?*" she'd say. She was angling, Ned could see, but it wasn't until later that he found out why.

"The first time she mentioned marriage I was

stunned," he said to Nancy. "I mean, she knew all about you and me. But I couldn't convince her that I was serious about you."

"Maybe you didn't try hard enough," Nancy said curtly.

"Oh, but I did. Jessica's smart, though. Every time I started talking about you she changed the subject. After a while I gave up, and then she *really* got into gear."

"Meaning?"

"Well, for instance, she constantly talked about our future together, as if it was already settled that we'd get married. And she came on to me physically in a very big way."

Nancy tensed up. She wasn't sure she wanted to hear about that. Nevertheless she asked, "So what happened?"

"Not what you think," Ned said with a grin. "I *did* get suspicious. Jessica was trying hard to land me. Too hard."

"So? Maybe she fell in love with you," Nancy said.

"I don't think so. She acts as if she loves me, but she's only pretending."

"Are you sure?"

"Positive."

Nancy frowned thoughtfully. "Well, if that's true, why does she want to marry you?"

"I don't know yet," Ned admitted. "But I have

the feeling she's up to no good. Maybe she's some kind of operator. If she is running a scam, I'll bet you anything she's run it before."

"What makes you so sure? Ned, so far you haven't got any hard evidence. In fact, you haven't got any evidence at all."

Ned smiled. "Oh, but I do! Did I mention that when I came across her that first day, she wasn't sweating?"

"So? What does that—oh, I see!" Nancy cried. "If she jogged all the way from downtown River Heights to your house, as she claimed, she should have been soaked with perspiration!"

"Exactly. There's something else, too—the day before that, a girl called my house and asked for me. But when I got on the phone and said hello she hung up."

"You think it was Jessica?"

"Definitely. I think she wanted to confirm my address."

Nancy nodded. "Sounds plausible. Any other clues?"

"Just one. Though it's really more of a hunch. Later that same day I went jogging. I got the feeling I was being followed, and sure enough, when I turned around, I spotted a car cruising behind me."

"Did you see the driver?"

"No, the sun was on the windshield. Too much glare. But I'm betting it was Jessica, checking out my habits."

"And when she realized that you went jogging every day, she hatched her plan to bump into you 'accidentally'?"

"Right. So, what do you think of my talents as a detective now, Nancy?"

"Not bad. But why the proposal?"

"Simple. I'm going to string her along until I can figure out her plan."

Her grin faded. "Are you sure that's the right thing to do? I mean, what if you're wrong? What if she genuinely wants to marry you? It's going to be hard to call it off. Uh, you *will* call it off, right?"

"Just as soon as I figure out what she's up to." Ned smiled sweetly. "Anyway, I don't think she really wants to marry me. I get the feeling I'm just a small part in some bigger plan she has, though I don't know what it could be yet."

"Okay, say she *is* up to something. Like, maybe she's interested in your family's money. Could—"

"But that can't be it. I've already ruled it out."

"Why?"

"For one thing, she's rich. She keeps plenty of cash in her purse, and her hotel bill is paid up—I saw her pay it. For another thing, I'm *not* rich—at least not very. If it's money she's after, she could do much better than me."

"But what about your dad's real estate business? And the cabin at Cedar Lake—not to mention the house on Merritt Island! Florida real estate is valuable."

Ned shook his head. "Lots of families have more assets than we do."

"I guess." Nancy paused a minute. "There's something that really bothers me, Ned. Why didn't you tell me about your crazy plan ahead of time?"

"I wanted to! I was going to explain everything at the pool party, but before I could you spilled the beans to Jessica about my proposal to you. She hit the roof. To keep her from getting suspicious, I had to make the announcement about my engagement to her."

"And just why *did* you propose to me the night before?"

Ned looked sheepish. "Well, it's kind of silly—"

"Maybe to you! But let me decide for myself."

"Okay. The truth is, a long time ago I promised myself that the first girl I ever proposed to would be Nancy Drew. When I realized that I'd have to ask Jessica to marry me, I decided to keep that promise anyway."

"Oh." Nancy's anger softened. "Tell me something else—did you know I'd turn you down?"

"I was pretty sure of it. As you said, it's too soon."

Leaning back, Nancy weighed everything he had told her. Part of her was still ticked off. If only she'd known in advance! It was sweet of him to have proposed to her first, but she would gladly have traded that proposal for some early warning from him about Jessica.

On the other hand, she was intrigued. If Ned was right and Jessica wasn't in love with him, then her determined pursuit of Ned was very suspicious. But they'd have to figure out *what* she was up to. Could it be something innocent? Not really, Nancy decided, because she'd have been able to confide in Ned then.

So Ned had to be right. . . .

"What's your plan?" Nancy asked. "Do you want me to help investigate Jessica?"

"Yes. In fact, I think she's expecting it. After all, you're a detective."

"*And* your jilted girlfriend." Nancy smiled. "I won't have any trouble acting that part."

"Good."

"What about your parents? And Bess and George? Can we let them in on it?"

Ned drummed his fingers on his knee. "Bess

41

and George, okay. It would be better to keep my parents in the dark, though."

"Ned, that's cruel. They're very upset," Nancy told him.

"I know, but they're not good actors the way you are, and Jessica will be seeing a lot of them in the next few weeks."

"I suppose you're right." Nancy didn't like that part of the plan, but it was necessary. Jessica must not suspect a thing. If she did, she would be gone like a shot before they'd had a chance to find out the truth about her.

Just then the hygienist entered the waiting room. "Mr. Nickerson? I'm sorry, but I still can't locate your records. We'll have to take new X-rays."

Ned looked confused. "You lost my X-rays?"

"I don't understand it." The woman sighed. "We're very careful. We return the X-rays to the files as soon as we're finished with them."

Nancy and Ned exchanged a look. "That's strange," he said.

"Why don't you come in now?" the dental assistant said.

"I'll be right there," Ned answered. Then he turned to Nancy and took her hand. "I'm really sorry you had to find out about Jessica the way you did. I didn't mean to hurt you, Nancy."

"I can see that now."

"Can you forgive me?"

"Well, anything's possible. . . ."

But she was only kidding. It was a relief to hear that Ned didn't really love Jessica. And she was proud of him for following his instincts too.

She wasn't totally sure he was right however. It still remained to be seen whether Jessica was up to no good.

As the hygienist wheeled around to leave, Ned rose to follow her. Nancy stopped him with a touch. "Ned?" she asked, "I want to know one more thing. What would you have done if I had said yes when you proposed to me?"

"What do you think?" Ned answered, smiling. Then, with a wink, he was gone.

For the next several days Nancy kept in touch with Ned by phone. He reported nothing unusual. To Nancy's frustration, Jessica gave no hint that she wanted anything more than to marry him, settle down in River Heights, and live happily ever after.

Then one day an invitation appeared in Nancy's mailbox. Jessica was throwing herself a bridal shower in her suite at the Royal Hotel. Nancy accepted with a short, formal letter of reply, then plotted her strategy with Bess and George. She had been told she could bring friends, so she invited them.

"You look great, Nan," George commented as they rode the hotel elevator up on the day of the shower. "That outfit is perfect—very elegant."

Nancy nodded. "Thanks. It's part of my plan. I want to upstage Jessica if I can."

"Exactly what I would do if I were the jilted girlfriend," Bess remarked.

"You got it. If I can make her believe that's what I am, she'll let down her guard. And I can find out just what she's up to."

"Quiet, you guys," George said. "We're here."

The elevator lurched to a halt on the fifteenth floor. The doors trundled open, and the girls heard the babble of conversation and the clink of tableware to their right.

"That way," Nancy said.

The shower was crowded. For a girl who was new to River Heights, Jessica had managed to acquire a lot of friends, Nancy saw. Girls were loading their plates with delicious-looking food at a buffet table. A white-jacketed waiter poured soda and juice in a corner. Nancy scanned the room for Jessica.

She was standing with Ned near a tall, round-topped window, looking radiant in a long summer dress of pastel blue cotton with a demure lace collar. As Nancy watched, she hugged Ned's arm and gazed up at him adoringly. She was the picture of a woman in love—all wide-eyed wonder and pink-cheeked excitement. Ned himself looked stony. His parents watched helplessly from nearby.

Then Jessica spotted Nancy. Whispering something to Ned, she left him and swept lightly across the room. "Nancy, I'm *sooo* glad you could come," she cooed as she drew near.

Nancy had a brief impulse to turn around and leave. But she reminded herself why she was there. . . .

"Hello, Jessica," she said stiffly. "I'm *sooo* glad you invited me."

"I simply had to! After all, you're one of Ned's dearest *friends,*" she said, pointedly stressing the word.

Nancy ignored the barb. "My, what a 'sweet' dress," she remarked coolly. "It makes you look so young and innocent."

Jessica smirked. She was ready for Nancy. "Oh, that's why I bought it. *Ned* says he hates it when girls try to look older than they are. He says it's immature."

"Really?" Nancy smoothed down her long white silk jacket. "That's odd. Ned told *me* he loves the sophisticated look. He said he likes girls who've got the *figure* to carry it off."

Two tiny red spots appeared on Jessica's

cheeks. She turned to Nancy's friends. "I'm sorry, I don't believe I got your names?"

"I'm Bess Marvin."

"George Fayne."

"George! How unusual! Your parents must have been expecting a boy."

"No, they named me Georgia. I got nick-named George when I was little, and it stuck."

"How terrible."

"Not really. I like my name."

"Well, are all those presents for me?" Jessica said, eyeing the smartly wrapped gifts each girl was holding.

Who else would they be for? Nancy thought to herself. Aloud she asked, "Where should we put them?"

"That table over there, but don't trouble your-selves. I'll carry them. Oh, Nancy, you don't mind if I open yours now, do you? I'm dying for a little preview—"

"Please. Go ahead, I don't mind."

At the gift table, Jessica unwrapped Nancy's box. Inside was a silver-backed hand mirror. "Oh, how lovely!"

"I thought you'd like it," Nancy said. "You strike me as the kind of girl who likes to look at herself a lot." It wasn't easy being this mean. But a job was a job.

"Why, you little—!"

Nancy's insult worked perfectly. Dropping the mirror on the table, Jessica spun and returned to Ned with an outraged cry.

"Nice going, Nan." George chuckled. "I'd never have believed you could play the part of a meanie so well."

"Yeah, you really got under her skin with that crack about the mirror," Bess agreed.

For the next hour Nancy concentrated on observing Jessica. It was frustrating because Jessica was acting the part of his fiancée perfectly. She never let down her guard. She looked thrilled and delighted to be engaged to Ned, and left his side only one time—to fix *him* a lavish ham sandwich at the buffet table.

Glumly Nancy watched Jessica dress the sandwich with cheese, lettuce, tomato, mustard, and a heap of olives. The case was beginning to look hopeless, she felt. Maybe Jessica wasn't faking her feelings for Ned.

Then, suddenly, an insight hit her like a jolt of electricity. Jessica was carrying the ham sandwich back to Ned. Of course! Why hadn't she realized it right away?

Crossing the room, Nancy approached Bess and George, who were talking to Ned's cousin, Helen Tyne. "Guys, can I see you in the hall?"

"What's up, Nan?" Bess asked once the three were outside.

Nancy could barely keep the excitement out of her voice. "Ned was right! Jessica isn't really in love with him!"

"Wow! Can you prove it?" George asked, surprised.

"Sure. What's the first thing people do when they fall in love?"

Bess shrugged. "I don't know. Shop for new clothes?"

"Slim down?" George offered.

"No! They find out everything they can about each other," Nancy observed.

"So?" Bess asked.

"So, get this—Jessica has known Ned for weeks, yet she hasn't learned one very basic fact about him—he hates olives!"

Chapter

Five

BESS AND GEORGE exchanged looks.

"That's it?" Bess asked after a pause. "Ned hates olives? That's all?"

"She piled a bunch on his sandwich! Don't you see what it means?" Nancy pressed.

"It probably means nothing. Maybe Ned never told her."

Nancy tapped her foot impatiently. "Oh, come on. They've been together just about every evening and weekend for a month."

"Well, maybe it just hasn't come up yet," George objected.

"You don't understand. This is basic. It's like finding out whether someone likes cream and sugar in their coffee. If you love them you notice that kind of thing right away."

"Well . . ." George didn't look convinced.

"Besides, they've gone to tons of restaurants together, according to Ned. By now she's had plenty of time to spot his food likes and dislikes."

"Okay, suppose you're right," Bess reasoned. "Where do you go from here? You can't arrest her for giving him olives."

"No," Nancy admitted. "But I think I may know why she's so anxious to marry Ned."

Her friends waited.

"Well, are you going to tell us the reason?" George asked.

"Not yet. It's only a guess now, and I want to check it out before I say anything. But if I'm right you two will be the first to know," Nancy promised. "After Ned, that is."

They were all called back inside then because Jessica was getting ready to open her presents.

Nancy went to the Nickersons' house the next morning. The neighborhood was as tranquil as ever, but inside the Nickerson home the mood was gloomy. Ned's mother looked drawn and pale. Ned's father—who was home from work—was storming around, looking furious.

Ned was at his father's office, luckily. If he had been at home, he might have been forced to tell his father everything, just to calm him down.

"That son of mine deserves a thrashing," Mr. Nickerson growled. He passed Nancy a plate of warm, buttery croissants. They were seated in the sunny breakfast nook. "I'm ashamed of him. His performance at that shower yesterday was disgraceful. He ignored you completely!"

Nancy bit her lip. She hated keeping Ned's parents in the dark. Ned's performance had been perfect—exactly as they had planned it. But she couldn't tell them. If they knew the truth their relief would show, and the change would definitely make Jessica suspicious.

"James, calm down," Ned's mother urged. "There must be a reason why Ned didn't speak to Nancy. Perhaps he was embarrassed."

"Well, he should be! Marrying that Thorne girl is a mistake."

"I'm afraid you're right." Mrs. Nickerson sighed. "I'm more convinced than ever that she doesn't make Ned *happy*. Did you notice how uneasy he looked yesterday, Nancy?"

Nancy spread jam on her croissant. "Yes, but a

lot of things could account for that. For one thing, it was a bridal shower. Guys aren't supposed to enjoy being put on display."

"But he didn't have to stay for the whole thing," Mrs. Nickerson pointed out. "Jessica shooed the men out before opening the presents."

"I know, but until then she made a huge fuss over Ned."

Mr. Nickerson stirred his coffee too briskly and some sloshed over the rim. "I wish I could talk some sense into him. Have you had any luck, Nancy?"

"Not really." Nancy dodged the question and looked down, concentrating too hard on her coffee. "I've been doing some thinking about Jessica, though, and I've got a question for you. Is Ned due to inherit a lot of money?"

Silence descended as the significance of her question sank in. Mr. Nickerson abruptly stopped stirring his coffee. "Are you saying Jessica's a gold digger?"

"No. But anything's possible with someone we all know so little about. She may hope to get rich someday."

Mr. Nickerson nodded. "Well, I'll admit that when we die Ned will be well off. But rich? I don't know. Some people may see it that way, but he won't be a millionaire."

"What about relatives?" Nancy asked. "Has anyone left Ned any money recently?"

Mrs. Nickerson thoughtfully shook her head. "No. Fortunately, no one has died on either side of the family in years."

"And even when they do, I doubt there will be much money in it for Ned," Mr. Nickerson added. "I'm sorry, Nancy."

Nancy hid her disappointment. Her theory wasn't panning out. "What about Jessica's parents? Did they die recently?" she asked.

"What would that have to do with it?" Mr. Nickerson wondered.

"Well, it's possible that they bequeathed her some money, but as a condition of the inheritance she has to be married."

"I see. Well, her parents *are* dead, but they didn't die all that recently. Her mother died of cancer a year ago; her father not long after that."

"Hmmm." Nancy thought that over. "Well, that probably kills my second theory. If I was right she would have married months ago."

"Maybe it's *not* true," Mrs. Nickerson said, leaning forward hopefully. "Maybe her parents aren't yet dead!"

Nancy shrugged. "No. That kind of story is easy to check. I doubt that she'd lie. Besides, why come all the way to River Heights for a husband? She could find one in Chicago."

Mrs. Nickerson looked crushed. "Too bad. I was hoping you had something we could use to open Ned's eyes."

"I'm afraid I don't. But I'll keep you posted."

Nancy chewed her croissant slowly. The truth was, things weren't as bleak as she had implied. Her theory wasn't dead—not quite yet. There was one more angle to check out.

Later at home Nancy dialed Emerson College, Ned's school. After a minute she was connected with Pat Burnett, Ned's basketball coach.

"Nancy, what a pleasure to hear from you!" Coach Burnett said. "How are you? I haven't seen you since you uncovered the reason for all those horrible practical jokes."

Nancy smiled sadly. The coach was referring to a case that she privately thought of as *Two Points to Murder*. Uncovering a practical joker's identity had proved tougher than she had imagined—and it had resulted in a painful breakup with Ned. She was glad that it was over.

"I'm fine, Mr. Burnett. I wonder if you could help me, though. I need some information that might be confidential."

"I'll help you if I can," the coach promised. "But knowing you, I'm sure you have a good reason for wanting the info."

"I do. Tell me, has Ned been approached by professional scouts, or has he had an offer to play professionally?"

The coach chuckled. "Football, baseball, or basketball?"

"Doesn't matter."

"Well, Ned is professional material in all three. But to answer your question, no. I don't believe he's had any offers. Not yet."

"Has there been any speculation in the newspapers?" Nancy asked. "Any stories that might lead someone to believe that Ned is going to turn pro and make a lot of money?"

"Not that I know of. Say, is Ned in some kind of trouble?"

"No, not at all," Nancy said. She thought to herself, But someone may be trying to hustle him because she thinks he's about to strike it rich.

"Well, if there's anything else I can do, just holler," the coach remarked. His tone lightened. "Now, will you be coming to visit this year? You know, you've got a front row seat waiting for you at every game."

"Thanks. I'll try to make it down for a couple of basketball games."

"Terrific! Look forward to seeing you."

Nancy said good-bye and hung up. She was beginning to get really discouraged. It looked as though money couldn't possibly be Jessica's motive. Ned just wasn't the right kind of target.

Could there be another reason why Jessica wanted to marry him? Nancy examined the question for several minutes, but came up empty.

Lifting the receiver again, she dialed Ned at his office.

"Hi, Nancy, can't talk right now," Ned said. "I'm finishing up some paperwork. But I've got some news for you. How about if we meet at noon? The fountain in the mall."

"Ned, that's dangerous," Nancy objected. "Aren't you supposed to meet Jessica at the mall around then?"

"At the jeweler's. The fountain's at the other end. She won't spot us."

"I don't know." Nancy bit her lip.

"Come on, Nancy, it'll be okay. Besides, I miss you. I want to see you."

Nancy felt her resolve melt. A smile lifted the corners of her mouth. "Now that you mention it, I sort of miss you too."

"Sort of? Is that all?"

"You nut! Of course not. See you at noon."

Nancy arrived early. She wanted to do some advance surveillance. Checking the area, she saw that the jewelry store was indeed at the opposite end of the mall. Furthermore, it was near the main entrance. If Jessica entered that way it was unlikely that she would spot them.

Satisfied, she walked to the far side of the fountain and sat at its edge. In spite of her care she was nervous. Meeting Ned in public was definitely a risk.

"Hi, gorgeous!" Leaning over, Ned planted a kiss on her cheek.

Nancy jumped. "You scared me!"

"Sorry, but you looked so pretty sitting there I couldn't resist."

"Ned, cut it out. We have to be careful," Nancy said cautiously.

"Don't worry. The fountain's hiding us."

Looking behind her, she saw that he was right. A circle of jets was pushing water high in the air. They were hidden from view.

She relaxed. "It's great to see you. I've got to talk to you." Wasting no time, she filled him in on her talk with his parents and her call to Pat Burnett. "This case is looking pretty hopeless, Ned," she finished gloomily.

"Not much to go on," Ned agreed. "But I'm not ready to drop it yet. In fact, I'm now more convinced than ever that she must be running some kind of a scam."

"Ned! What happened? You know something!" Nancy grabbed his sleeve. "Come on, quit holding out!"

Ned grinned at her. "Do I get a kiss for this?"

"Ned!" Nancy rolled her eyes.

"Here's what happened. I met Jessica for lunch at the Royal yesterday. We were sitting at the table when one of the waiters came up to her with a telephone. She had an urgent call. But she wouldn't take it in front of me—she insisted on telling the person that she'd call them right back from the pay phone in the lobby. She told me it was her aunt calling from Detroit, but I could hear the voice, just faintly, over the receiver, and it was definitely a man. And he was shouting."

"So you followed her and listened to the conversation?" Nancy asked.

"Yeah, and you wouldn't believe the change in her! She was practically screaming into the phone. She was so furious I don't think she would have noticed me if I'd walked up and tapped her on the shoulder. 'Stop hounding me!' she kept yelling. 'I already told you, you'll get it. In fact, I'm working on it right this second, if only you'd let me get back to what I'm doing. And don't call me again, or you'll blow everything!' Then she slammed down the receiver and I had to hustle back to our table before she saw me."

"Wow." Nancy was overjoyed. "She must have been talking to a creditor. So she really *is* up to something!"

"Right." Ned nodded. "The only thing is, that phone call may convince you and me, but it isn't solid proof."

"Hmmm. Tell me something, Ned. Has she asked you for a loan?"

"No," he told her. "She could be holding off. Maybe she wants to build up my trust."

Nancy groaned. "Great. At the rate she's moving you'll be married before we get any evidence."

"Don't sweat it," Ned said with a grin. "I think I've come up with a way to test our theory."

"How?"

"Temptation. I'm going to offer her a gift and see if she grabs for it. If she does, it'll be evidence that she's out for money."

"Sounds good. What's the present?"

Ned smiled mysteriously. "I'll tell you later. Right now I want to make up for lost time." He slipped his arms around her.

"Make it quick," Nancy urged. "It's almost time for you to meet Jessica."

Ned complied. Moving close, he kissed her. It felt wonderful. Nancy wrapped her arms around him and kissed him back with days and days' worth of pent-up feelings.

They were still locked together that way when the fountain was abruptly shut off. Like a theater curtain going down, the geysers fell to the pool's surface with a *splat*.

It was quiet. Nancy and Ned were exposed for all the mall to see. They moved apart, but not in time. From the other side of the fountain, a girl's voice rose in fury.

"Ned Nickerson, what's going on here?"

It was Jessica!

Chapter

Six

Eyes blazing, Jessica marched around the fountain. There wasn't time to invent a cover story, Nancy realized. She and Ned would have to wing it and hope for the best.

"J-Jessica!" Ned stammered. "I thought we were meeting at the jeweler's!"

"I got here early and decided to do some window-shopping," Jessica said. "Now, what's going on here?"

"Nancy and I were talking—"

"You were not! You were kissing. I saw you, and I want an explanation."

Ned cleared his throat. "Okay, if you insist. I was, uh—saying good-bye to Nancy. This is our final farewell."

Jessica snorted. "Oh, come on. Do you expect me to believe that?"

"Sure. It's true. Nancy never accepted that *our* engagement was real—until this afternoon. Now I've finally convinced her that it's over between her and me."

"So, what was that kiss? A consolation prize?"

"No, it was our farewell kiss. Right, Nancy?"

"I—I suppose."

"I don't know," Jessica said suspiciously. "It didn't look like 'farewell' to me. It looked more friendly than that."

They were in trouble. Jessica didn't believe the story, Nancy realized. They needed to make it more convincing—but how?

Suddenly she remembered a trick she had learned in an acting class. She shut her eyes and concentrated for a second, until she felt the tears swelling up behind her closed lids. Then, glaring at Jessica, she suddenly hissed, "You're horrible! I'm going to make you pay!"

Jessica was taken aback. "Huh? What for? What are you talking about?"

"Me and Ned." Nancy pretended to work herself into a rage. "The two of us had something really special—until *you* came along!"

"Oh, I get it. You think I stole him." Jessica gleefully took the bait. "Well, I've got news for you. Stealing isn't my style. You lost him. You didn't try hard enough."

"That's not true. I *love* him!" Nancy wailed loudly.

"Sorry. The game's over." Jessica was completely hooked. She rubbed in her victory. "Ned's mine, so you'd better get used to it." Turning to him, she commanded, "Let's go. Aren't we supposed to be looking at *wedding rings*?"

"Yes. Well, good-bye, Nancy," Ned said, rising from his seat.

They had done it! Jessica had swallowed the lie hook, line, and sinker. Nancy knew she should drop the act and clear out, but she couldn't resist going one step further.

"Ned! You can't leave me like this!" she cried pitifully. Leaping up, she grabbed his arm.

"Nancy, it's over," Ned stated.

"No. Just give me a second chance! Things will be different, I swear!"

"Forget it. Let go of my arm—*you're overdoing it!*" he hissed directly into her ear so Jessica wouldn't hear.

But Nancy held on. She was enjoying herself. It was the most fun she had had in ages. Tears were flowing freely down her cheeks. Curious bystanders had gathered in a circle. She appealed to them with red-rimmed eyes.

Jessica, meanwhile, was furious. Her eyes blazed with possessive fury. Stepping close to Nancy, she said, "Let go of him. It's over."

"No!"

"Okay, you asked for it—"

Reaching over, she pried Nancy's fingers loose, then shoved her hard. Nancy teetered backward —and fell into the fountain!

Water closed in over her head. Nancy held her breath, scrambled to her feet, and rose, sputtering. She was soaked from head to toe. Wet strands of hair clung to her face.

"That was unfair!" she shouted.

"Maybe. But next time you'll think twice before you touch my fiancé. Come on, Ned." Jessica pulled him away.

A maintenance man helped Nancy from the pool. On the floor nearby was an underwater vacuum hose. It was he who had turned off the water to clean the fountain, she realized.

"Are you okay, miss?" the man asked in concern. "She shoved you awfully hard."

Nancy raked back her hair with her fingers and checked to be sure that Jessica and Ned were out of earshot.

They were.

She laughed. "Believe me, I've never felt better!"

Two hours later Nancy was three thousand feet in the air. Smiling, she eased forward the wheel of her rented Cessna, reduced the throttle to cruising speed and, after a moment, adjusted the trim tab control next to her seat.

Nancy loved flying. She and Ned had taken lessons together, but that wasn't the only reason. There was something magical about soaring far above the ground. She enjoyed watching the checkerboard fields and ribbonlike roads below. It made her problems seem smaller.

It also helped her to think, which was what she needed to do right then. Her investigation was getting nowhere fast, she knew. She needed some fresh ideas.

Nancy pondered the problem for almost an hour. As she did she flew a large circle around River Heights. Below her she picked out familiar landmarks: the rivers, the interstate, downtown —even the green fairways of the country club. Surrounding it all, like an enormous flat pancake, were countless miles of fields and farms. River Heights was a growing city, but its roots were firmly embedded in midwestern soil.

Finally, satisfied with her new plan, Nancy

headed back to the airport. Descending to eight hundred feet, she smoothly slipped into the rectangular landing pattern, glided through the base leg turns, and dropped onto the runway for a three-point landing.

Once off the field, Nancy taxied to a parking place, cut the engine, chocked the wheels, tethered the wings, and locked the cabin. She was walking toward a hangar to pay for her ride when she noticed another rental plane rolling in. Sunlight flashed on its windshield, but then the plane turned and she could see in the cockpit. She recognized the pilot instantly.

Jessica!

Nancy watched, dumbfounded, as Jessica ran through the same postlanding procedure that she herself had just completed. Jessica had her pilot's license? That was a surprise. In some ways, though, it fit, she realized. Flying required discipline and cool-headed logic, and those qualities could easily describe Jessica.

When she was finished securing the plane, Jessica walked over to Nancy. "Before *you* say anything, I want to apologize. I'm sorry I pushed you in the fountain. I got carried away."

"It happens," Nancy said coolly. "I'm afraid I got carried away myself."

"Understandable." Jessica smiled. "Ned must be tough to give up."

"You said it."

"How long have you had your license?" Jessica asked, quickly changing the subject.

"A year. How about you?"

"Two."

"Fly much?"

"Oh, every chance I get. I just love it, don't you?"

Nancy felt odd. It was strange to share a hobby with someone like Jessica. She thought of them as total opposites.

"Do you skydive too?" Jessica asked.

Nancy was stunned. "As a matter of fact, I do."

"Really? How many jumps have you made?"

"About thirty."

"I've done fifty-two." Jessica smiled again, and this time Nancy caught a flicker of smug satisfaction in it.

"You know," Jessica continued, her voice now bright and false, "I was planning to go up for a jump this afternoon. Care to go with me?"

Nancy hesitated. There was nothing she wanted less than to go skydiving with Jessica, but at the same time she was tempted. There was a subtle dare implied in Jessica's offer.

"Of course, if you're not *up* to it—"

"Oh, I'm up to it. Let's go."

When they had paid for their planes, Nancy

and Jessica walked to the office of the River Heights Skydiving Academy, rented equipment, and hired a pilot. Then they went inside and went to work at separate tables.

Carefully, Nancy stretched her chute on a long, narrow packing table and checked its gores, seams, and suspension lines. She pleated the canopy and slid the deployment sleeve over it. Next she folded the suspension lines zigzag fashion. It was a tedious routine, but she followed it methodically. Caution was the key to safe parachuting.

When the lines and canopy were accordion-pleated in a pile, she attached the sleeve retainer line, pilot chute cord, and pilot chute—the miniparachute that would whisk the main canopy from her pack. Then she squashed the whole pile into its square container and fastened it with four ripcord pins.

The hard part was over. Still working carefully, she attached the pack opening bands and checked her harness to see that the ripcord was clear. She was done first and went into the women's changing room. She pulled on a one-piece jumpsuit, boots, and gloves, and tucked her bubble-style goggles into her visorless helmet. Then she went back into the packing room to don her chute and reserve chute, which together weighed forty pounds. She felt like an elephant.

Outside, Nancy and Jessica discussed the jump. Jessica wanted to exit from eight thousand feet, giving them thirty seconds of free-fall. Nancy didn't like the idea. She knew that up in the sky thirty seconds could feel like an eternity.

Besides, she had never jumped from that great a height. Nevertheless, she agreed. She didn't want to appear timid.

A few minutes later they were in the air. Nancy squatted nervously on the bench. She had long ago gotten over the "six-jump slump"—the paralyzing fear that every novice feels after the exhilaration of the first few jumps. But she still had butterflies. It was normal.

She was also careful to keep the ripcord handle on her reserve chute covered with her left hand. If the handle caught on anything and the reserve fell open, the chute would be sucked out of the plane in no time. And she would be sucked out with it. People had lost limbs that way.

As they approached their exit point, Jessica tapped Nancy on the shoulder. "Want a last-minute check?" she asked over the roar of the engine.

"No, thanks." Nancy shook her head. A last-minute check was standard procedure, but she didn't want Jessica anywhere near her pack. She didn't trust her.

Finally they were on their approach. Nancy

went to the open doorway on the starboard side of the plane. Icy wind whistled by her face. Gripping the handles on either side of the doorway, she checked their position. On the ground a mile and a half below was a tiny drop zone with an even tinier white X in the middle. That was their target.

Using hand signals so that she would not be misunderstood, she signaled for the pilot to circle to their exit point once again, this time moving five degrees to the left. He did. When they were almost there, Nancy glanced over her shoulder at Jessica. "Ready?"

Jessica nodded. There was a gleam in her eyes and a confident smile on her face. She was enjoying the effect of eight thousand feet on Ned's ex-girlfriend, Nancy could see. She might even be hoping that Nancy would be unable to handle it—that she would panic and deploy early, or pull her ripcord when she was out of position.

Both mistakes could be fatal, Nancy knew, but if that was what Jessica was hoping for she was going to be disappointed. As they approached the exit point she shouted to the pilot.

"Cut!"

The pilot cut the engine. Nancy waited a second, braced her feet, then bravely launched herself headfirst out the doorway.

Falling. As always, for the first few seconds Nancy felt nothing but an overpowering combination of terror and ecstasy. Then the wind was whistling in her helmet; tugging savagely at her jumpsuit. The terror fell away and she felt sensational. She was flying! Her heart hammered.

She checked her body position—good. She was in a perfect "frog." She was a little to the right of her course, though. Twisting her body, she soared off to the left.

Where was Jessica? Somewhere above her, no doubt. Had she, too, made a headfirst door exit? Nancy smiled to herself. No way Jessica had topped her in that!

The ground grew closer. Regretfully, Nancy tested her O.A.J., Opening Altitude Judgment. Was it time to pull? She wanted to deploy at exactly twenty-five hundred feet. From there it was an easy glide to the drop zone.

At last she decided to pull. Counting, she arched—looked—reached for the ripcord handle—pulled.

But nothing happened! There was no flutter, no opening shock. Paralyzed, Nancy realized that her chute had failed. She was still falling at terminal velocity.

In eighteen seconds she would hit the ground.

Chapter

Seven

18...

Nancy fought down her panic. There was plenty of time to decide what to do. What were her options? Her chute wasn't going to open, that much was clear.

17...

She would have to deploy her reserve. Clamping her legs together, she reached for the handle —then hesitated. The reserve was dangerous—

16...

It was difficult to deploy and once open it

would suspend her upside down. When she reached the ground she could break a leg, or her back.

15 . . .

But she had no other choice. Glancing down, she gripped the reserve ripcord handle . . .

14 . . .

And pulled. Nothing happened!

13 . . .

Panic gripped her. She wanted to scream. But as the sound rose in her throat she choked it off. There was no time for hysterics. Think, she told herself.

12 . . .

Deliberately, she forced herself to glance down again. The reserve ripcord handle was still in place. She had to pull it hard, with almost twenty pounds of pressure, she remembered.

11 . . .

She pulled it again. The cord moved several inches, but the compartment didn't open. She was about to tug it again when an object to her left caught her attention—

10 . . .

Jessica! What was she doing? She should have pulled her ripcord long ago. Nancy watched, frozen, as Jessica sailed expertly toward her.

9 . . .

73

She was pointing toward Nancy's pack. She could see the problem, Nancy realized, and she was going to try to fix it.

8 . . .

Jessica maneuvered close. Nancy wanted to wave her away, but it was too late to deploy her reserve chute. It might open under Jessica and collapse. Then both of them would fall to their deaths.

7 . . .

Jessica was right next to her. Reaching over, she jerked at the pack on Nancy's back.

6 . . .

No luck. Nothing happened.

5 . . .

Jessica jerked again. Hurry! Nancy thought. The ground was very close. She could see cars on a road—

4 . . .

Cows in a field. Jessica jerked again. This time, something ripped.

3 . . .

A fluttering. Then suddenly—

2 . . .

Nancy's harness yanked her hard, dropping her rudely into an upright position. Her chute was open! She was safe!

Glancing down, she saw that Jessica's chute

was open too. Jessica was fifty feet below her, steering to the right.

Nancy looked down. She was only three hundred feet off the ground. There wasn't much time to move around. She'd have to make the best landing she could.

Fortunately, they were over a field. Something was growing in it, but Nancy couldn't tell what. All she could see were rows of small plants. They looked like green corduroy.

The ground was soft. Nancy automatically rolled into the familiar parachute-landing fall, but it was hardly necessary. The soil cushioned her impact. She quickly stood up, collapsed her chute, and stepped out of her harness.

Jessica came running over. "Nancy, are you all right?"

Nancy pulled off her helmet. "I'll live. What was wrong with my chute?"

"One of the opening bands was crossed over to the opposite side. You must have hooked it on wrong when you packed."

Nancy understood. The band had kept the pilot chute inside the pack, even after the ripcord pins had been pulled.

"Thanks for saving me," Nancy said.

"I'm just glad you're okay."

But she wasn't. Suddenly she was shaking all

over. She sat down on the ground. It wasn't delayed fear that was getting her, it was a realization—she *hadn't* made a mistake. She remembered hooking up the opening bands. She had done it perfectly. And that could mean only one thing. . . .

"Jessica tried to *kill* you?" Bess asked in disbelief.

It was several hours later. Nancy was at home. Dinner was over, and she was cleaning her room. Bess and George were sitting on her bed, their mouths hanging open.

"That's not exactly what I said," Nancy replied. "I said she sabotaged my chute."

"But when?" George asked. "You just told us that you packed it yourself. And you didn't let her do an equipment check."

"She fixed it when I was putting on my jumpsuit in the women's changing room."

Bess's features squeezed into a look of pure hatred. "That creep!"

"Can you prove anything?" George asked her.

Nancy scooped up a pair of jeans from the floor and folded them. "No, that's the problem. I didn't see her do it."

"But you *know* she's guilty!" Bess cried.

"Sure, but I don't have any evidence. If I

accuse her she'll just deny it. Anyway, I can't accuse her because she saved my life, remember?" Nancy's tone was ironic.

George shook her head. "That's another thing I don't understand. After going to the trouble of sabotaging your chute, why did she bother to fix it in midair?"

"I'm not quite sure," Nancy said, taking some files from her desk and stuffing them in her file cabinet. "I have a theory though. I think she was getting her kicks."

"Some kicks. That was attempted murder!" Bess declared.

"Not really," Nancy said. "After all, I had a reserve chute. The chances that I would die were pretty slim."

"But kicks?" George asked. "Come on, isn't it more likely that she wanted to look like a hero? To make Ned proud?"

"Maybe, but I don't think so. After all, she could have been killed too! I think she did it for thrills. I think she genuinely enjoyed toying with my life."

"That's pretty weird," George remarked.

Bess had a stronger opinion. "It's downright sick. She's crazy."

Nancy disagreed, but said nothing. In her judgment, Jessica was far from crazy. She was smart, daring, and a skillful planner. That made her very dangerous.

But how could she prove it? Musing, she continued cleaning her room. There were shoes under her bed and a couple of articles of clothing scattered. In the excitement of the last two days she had totally abandoned her usual tidy habits.

At least she had a new plan to look forward to. If she was lucky, the following day would yield some evidence.

If not—

Just then Hannah knocked at her door. "Nancy? You have a visitor."

"Thanks. Show whoever it is up, will you?" Nancy called.

It was Jessica. If she was feeling the strain of having opened her parachute only a few hundred feet off the ground, she didn't show it. She looked cool, calm, collected, and very pretty in a simple but expensive-looking shirtdress.

"I dropped by to see how you're doing," Jessica said as she breezed into Nancy's room. "Are you okay? Can I get you anything?"

"For heaven's sake, I'm okay," Nancy answered more peevishly than she had intended.

"Of course you are. Still, you had a pretty close call. Hi, George, Bess," she said. "Did Nancy tell you about her 'adventure'?"

They nodded only, not trusting themselves to speak. George knew she'd tell Jessica off.

Nancy thought about the reserve parachute that she could have deployed if Jessica hadn't flown near. It *had* been a close call—thanks to Jessica's "heroics."

"Thanks again for helping me," Nancy forced herself to say.

"You're welcome. You know, this is a lovely room. You'll have to help me decorate our place after Ned and I get married."

Only a small muscle moving in and out near her jaw indicated how angry Nancy was. Even though she knew that Ned had no intention of marrying Jessica, it was an effort to keep her temper.

Jessica looked around. Spotting a framed photo of Ned on Nancy's dresser, she crossed the room and picked it up.

Nancy waited for her to comment, but the dark-haired girl said nothing. Instead, she set the photo down and glanced at the top of Nancy's desk, where several files on old cases still lay.

"Oh, are those notes on your cases?" Jessica

asked brightly. "How interesting. You must know all kinds of secrets."

She marched to the desk, her hand outstretched. Quickly Nancy dashed to intercept her. She scooped up the files before Jessica could open them. So that was why Jessica had come to visit! Nancy thought. She wanted to snoop.

"I know a few secrets, sure," Nancy said, quickly stuffing the files in a drawer. One of them contained her notes on Jessica. "But secrets are for keeping. If I told them I'd lose my credibility. No one would bring me any cases."

"Naturally. How silly of me," Jessica said. She looked disappointed that she had not managed to peek at the contents of the files.

A horn sounded in Nancy's driveway. Startled, all four girls turned their heads toward the window. Jessica walked over and looked out.

"It's Ned! What's he doing here?" she wondered suspiciously.

Nancy wondered the same thing. After what had happened in the mall that morning he should have known better than to risk coming to her house.

But wait—he *did* know better, Nancy realized. That meant he was springing his trap! Ned was planning to offer Jessica an expensive gift. If she accepted it, they'd know that part of her motive for marrying him was money. Maybe all of her motive.

Nancy crossed to the window too—and froze. She couldn't believe it. The "gift" Ned had chosen as bait was far more lavish than anything she had ever imagined.

It was a brand-new car!

Chapter

Eight

N ED, WHAT ARE you doing here?" Jessica asked as they walked out Nancy's front door. She tried to sound pleasantly surprised, but Nancy could tell that she was furious.

"Looking for you," he explained. "You weren't at the Royal, so I did a little detective work and tracked you down."

"Oh, really?" Jessica obviously didn't believe him. The scene at the fountain had left a seed of doubt. "How?"

"I talked to the attendant in the hotel parking

garage. He said that you asked for directions to
this street."

"So you figured I had gone to see Nancy."

"Exactly. Well, what do you think of it?" he
asked, patting the hood of the car.

Jessica looked it over. It was a hot-pink sports
model with a sunroof, a stereo, and air-
conditioning.

"It's beautiful, but that's not exactly a color I
thought you'd go for."

Ned smiled, all innocence. "Oh, it's not for
me, it's for you."

"For me?"

"Surprised? I thought it was time you stopped
driving a rental car, so I picked this out."

Jessica's pretty, cupid's-bow mouth dropped
open. "Ned, are you serious? You went out and
bought me a car?"

"Well, I haven't paid for it yet, but if you like
it, I'll put down a deposit."

"Wait a minute—if you haven't paid for it,
then how did you get it here?"

"Test drive," he said proudly.

Slowly, Jessica walked around the car, watching avidly as Ned pointed out its features. She
threw a little grin at Nancy, and Nancy scowled
back at her, pretending to be furious.

Jessica's eyes were gleaming. From greed?

Nancy wondered. "Ned, I simply can't believe this. Will you really buy this car for me?"

"Just say the word."

Jessica glanced at Nancy again, hesitating. "I—I don't know."

"Look, you *need* a car."

"True, but you're still in college. How will you make the payments?"

"Don't worry about that. Come on, Jessica, what do you say? Let me buy it for you. I want you to have it."

Nancy spun around, unable to hide her smile. Ned should have sold cars for the summer instead of insurance.

Once more Jessica circled the car. Nancy turned back, her expression under control. She was curious to see what Jessica would do. Would she ask Ned to buy it?

Jessica slid behind the wheel and ran her hands over the dashboard and the bucket seats. "Ned, it's wonderful."

"Then you want it?"

"No, take it back."

Ned was dumbfounded. "But—"

"I mean it, Ned. We can't afford it right now."

Nancy was astonished. She had been sure that Jessica would go for the car. Evidently so had Ned. He kept trying to persuade her to take it.

"Jessica, don't you like the color?"

"Of course I do, but I can't accept this car. We're just starting out. We have to save money."

"But—but—"

"My mind's made up. Take it back."

Late that evening Nancy phoned Ned. He had a telephone in his room, with his own private line. They didn't have to worry that his parents would find out.

"Nice try," she said, trying to console him.

"Thanks." Ned sighed. "You know, I was sure she would take the car."

"Me too. Well, either she guessed it might be a plant, or she really meant all that stuff about starting out and saving money."

Ned was skeptical. "No. What she said was only a cover. I'm positive of it."

"I think so too. But we have no facts to back up our feelings."

Leaning back against her pillows, Nancy discussed Jessica with him for several more minutes. Then she told him about her nearly fatal skydiving "accident." Ned was silent for a minute.

"If anything had happened to you—"

"Luckily, nothing did. And listen, I've got a plan for tomorrow."

She told him the details.

"Great!" he said enthusiastically. "Tell you what, I'll help out by inviting her to The Greenery for lunch."

"Poor Ned." Nancy chuckled. "Working undercover is *sooo* difficult."

Ned laughed. "Yeah, I just might die of boredom. Seriously, Nancy, either I break my engagement or we wrap this up soon. I don't want you in any more danger."

"I'll survive. It's time that I'm worried about. We're running out of it."

"We are?"

Nancy was confused. "Aren't we? Haven't you and Jessica set a wedding date?"

"Not yet. I brought up the subject the other day, but she brushed it off."

"That's strange. I thought she'd want to tie the knot as soon as possible. How come she's not in a hurry?"

"Good question."

For several minutes more they speculated. Then, finally, they said a tender good night. Nancy hung up and switched off her bedside light, but she didn't sleep well. All night she dreamed that she was falling through a bright blue sky. . . .

* * *

The next morning was gray and rainy. It was just as well. The rain gave Nancy an excuse to walk into the Royal Hotel well disguised. A trenchcoat concealed her slender figure, and a large floppy rain hat hid her face.

Pete Gomez, the hotel's manager and an old friend of Nancy's, was glad to see her. He offered his hand as she entered his office. "Nancy, it's a pleasure. I'm afraid I haven't got any missing jewels for you to track down today though."

Nancy smiled. She had endeared herself to Pete when she had recovered a five-carat diamond that a guest had claimed was stolen by a member of the hotel staff. It hadn't been stolen at all, as it turned out. The guest had faked the theft in order to make an insurance claim. She had hidden the diamond in a bar of soap.

"That's okay. I've got another reason for dropping by," she told him, sitting down. "I want a job."

Pete sat behind his desk and pulled out an employment application. "You got it. What do you want to be? Receptionist? Waitress in the Towers Lounge?"

Nancy grinned. "Guess again."

"House detective?"

"No! I want to be a chambermaid."

"But, Nancy, that's our lowest-paying position!" Pete looked dismayed. "Believe me, you'll make better money in the lounge."

"That's okay. I don't want any pay. In fact, I only want the job for one hour. There's a certain room I want to make up."

"Ah." Understanding dawned in Pete's eyes. "Which room?"

She told him.

"Oh, Jessica Thorne," he said, nodding. "She's one guest I could do without."

"Problems?" Nancy asked.

"You better believe it. She keeps room service in a frenzy. Nothing is ever good enough for her. One time she even told them to bring her new sugar packets for her coffee. She said the ones she got tasted funny."

"That's ridiculous."

"Of course it is, but she's a guest so we've got to please her. My theory is that she just likes to be waited on."

Nancy mulled over this new information. Jessica sounded like a pest. What she didn't sound like, however, was a girl who was concerned about saving money. New clothes, meals out, room service—that stuff added up.

"So, can you give me that chambermaid's job?" she asked.

Pete frowned. "Searching a guest's belongings

is against hotel policy—but I guess it can be arranged."

"I appreciate your help."

Pete took her to the office of Wanda Lewis, who was in charge of maid service. Soon Nancy was outfitted with a uniform and a cart. At five minutes past twelve—when Jessica, she knew, was lunching with Ned—Nancy pushed the cart off the service elevator onto the fifteenth floor.

Jessica's suite was just as she remembered it from the bridal shower. The shower gifts were still there, too, carelessly thrown under a table. Quickly, Nancy changed the sheets and towels, vacuumed, and ran through the rest of the routine that Mrs. Lewis had described. Then she went to work.

She started in the bathroom. Jessica's makeup was plentiful and expensive. She had dozens of shampoos, conditioners, and skin-care products. The medicine cabinet held nothing unusual except prescription sleeping pills. Did Jessica have trouble sleeping? Evidently not, Nancy decided. The bottle was still filled to the top.

Leaving the bathroom, she went to Jessica's closet. Nothing there except clothes. She checked the pockets: empty, except for a few crumpled gum wrappers. Jessica's dresser held mostly underwear, but in the top drawer Nancy found a purse. It contained a thousand dollars in cash and—she was in luck—Jessica's Illinois driver's license. Nancy copied down her Chicago address from it.

Next, she searched the desk. She was looking for a diary, letters, a checkbook—anything that might give her a clue what Jessica was doing in River Heights. But there was nothing. All she found was an old envelope filled with newspaper clippings. Whatever was inside the envelope originally had apparently been mailed to a Scott O'Malley—at an address in Chicago also. The return address was that of a law firm in Billings, Montana. Nancy pulled out one of the clippings to examine it.

She couldn't believe her eyes. It was a picture of Ned—from the past spring, when he'd broken his right arm and been pulled from his position as starting pitcher for Emerson College.

The story had run in many midwestern newspapers. Emerson's baseball team was hot, and the loss of their star pitcher was therefore big news. Why had Jessica cut out the photo?

One by one Nancy looked at the other clippings and with each one her heart beat faster.

They were all photos clipped from newspaper sports pages—photos of tall, dark-haired, square-jawed boys. Each boy slightly resembled Ned—

And every photo, except his, had a sinister black *X* drawn through it!

Chapter
Nine

WHAT DID THE X's mean? Scooping up the clippings, Nancy crossed the room. She sat on the edge of the bed and examined them more closely. There was no other writing on them, no notes, no identification. She checked the reverse sides of the pictures. Most had fragments of articles on them. Maybe she could use the articles to trace the photos. And what then?

Perhaps the boys in the photos had all been Jessica's victims. If so, what had she done to them? Nancy had no idea, but she didn't like the possibilities that came to mind. Another question: Why did they all look alike?

Suddenly she froze. A key was turning in the lock!

Jessica was back. Leaping up, Nancy stuffed the photos back in the envelope and threw the envelope in her maid's cart. Grabbing a fresh towel from the cart, she quickly tied it around her reddish gold hair. Then she snatched a rag and a can of wood polish and dove under a coffee table.

She was busily polishing the table's legs when Jessica marched in. "Oh, terrific," Ned's fiancée growled. "Just what I need. Aren't you done yet?"

"Sí. Soon, senorita," Nancy said, faking a Spanish accent.

"Well, make it snappy. This room should have been finished hours ago."

"Sí, sí."

Nancy polished harder, but did not emerge from under the coffee table. As long as she stayed underneath it, Jessica could not see her face. She waited, rubbing the wood to a high gloss, until Jessica went into her bathroom.

Quick as a flash, Nancy rose, pitched the rag and polish into her cart, and pushed it toward the door. She was halfway into the hall when she heard the bathroom door snap open behind her.

"Wait a minute. Where are you going?" Jessica demanded.

Nancy's heart pounded. She forced herself to stay calm. Without turning around, she contritely mumbled, "Senorita?"

"You forgot to give me a fresh bath mat."

"Oh, sorry. No more. Will bring one right away."

"Hurry up. I just had the most *booooring* lunch of my life, and I want to relax in the bath," Jessica said testily.

Without another word, Nancy hurried away. When she heard Jessica's door close behind her, she grinned. If Jessica found Ned "booooring," she couldn't really be planning to marry him, could she? But what *was* she planning to do with him?

The River Heights *Morning Record* was published only two blocks away from the Royal Hotel. Nancy threaded her way easily through its offices until she came to a door marked Morgue.

Knocking lightly, she pushed it open. "Mr. Pike? Are you here?"

A white-haired man wearing a yellow shirt, red suspenders, and seersucker pants peered around the end of a freestanding shelf. Ed Pike had been the staff researcher for the *Record* for almost forty years. His eyes lit up.

"Nancy Drew! Come on in. I haven't seen you in a dog's age."

"How've you been, Mr. Pike?"

"Fine, fine. What can I do for you?"

Nancy showed him the clippings. "Could you possibly tell me which newspapers published these shots? I want to contact those boys."

"That's a tall order." Mr. Pike looked the clippings over. As Nancy had done, he examined their reverse sides. "Hold on—some of these stories have datelines," he said.

"Then you can trace them?"

"I can try. Give me a day or two—say, what do those *X*'s mean?" he asked, squinting as he turned one of the clippings over.

"That's one of the things I'm hoping to find out," Nancy said.

"I get it. Another mystery, huh?"

"Yes, a real puzzler."

"You'll crack it," Mr. Pike said confidently. "You always do. By the way, have I ever showed you your morgue file?"

Mr. Pike maintained a file of all the stories the *Record* had ever run about her exploits. Nancy had seen it before, but she knew it was useless to point that out. Mr. Pike showed her the file every time she visited him.

In fact, he was already on his way to the file

drawer marked *D*. "Now where is that thing—here it is," he said, proudly pulling it out.

It was an inch thick. Nancy nodded in appreciation. She didn't care much about publicity, except when it brought new cases her way, but that day she couldn't help harboring a hope. She hoped that soon—very soon—that file would become one story thicker.

The following morning she drove to Chicago, taking the expressway into the center of the city.

It was time to get more information—and she was going to start at the address on Jessica's driver's license.

She found the street easily. It was an elegant avenue near the exclusive Lake Shore Drive. Large town houses stood on either side, many of them guarded by tall wrought-iron fences. Nancy parked, then walked up the sidewalk.

She couldn't find the house she was looking for. Checking a scrap of paper, she wondered if she had copied the number wrong. Then, suddenly, a car tooted its horn. Looking up, she saw that she was blocking the gate to a driveway.

She stepped out of the way. The gate must have been electronic, she realized, because it swung open automatically. As it did, a Mercedes turned in from the street.

Fortunately, the gates did not reclose. Nancy

watched as a distinguished-looking man un-loaded bags of groceries from the trunk of the Mercedes. Nancy walked up to him.

"Excuse me. Can you tell me which house is number twelve forty-seven?"

The man turned and studied her in surprise. He had lively brown eyes, a receding hairline, and the most rigid posture Nancy had ever seen.

"This is number twelve forty-seven," he said. "Can I help you?" He had a faint British accent.

"I hope so," Nancy said. "I need some infor-mation about a girl who may live here or may have lived here in the past. Her name is Jessica Thorne."

The man closed the trunk of the Mercedes with a thump. "The Thornes don't live here anymore. Mr. and Mrs. Thorne are dead."

"Well, it's their daughter I'm interested in."

"Hmmm." The man lifted a bag of groceries in each arm.

"Can you tell me about her?"

"I'm not sure that I should," he said, walking toward a side entrance. "Why do you want to know about her?"

Nancy launched into her prepared story. "A friend of mine is engaged to her, but his family isn't sure that she's right for him. I told them I'd check her out."

It was part of the truth.

The man stopped at the side door, juggled some keys, and opened it. "All right, then, come along inside. After I finish bringing in the groceries I'll fill you in."

A few minutes later Nancy was seated at a table in the kitchen. The room was enormous. It had a huge oven, a glass-fronted refrigerator, and a work island with a rack of heavy copper pots and pans hanging over it.

The man set a glass of iced tea in front of her. "Lemon?"

"Thanks," Nancy said. "Tell me, how did you know Jessica? Are you a family friend?"

"You could say that," the man replied, smiling faintly. He handed her a wedge of lemon. "I was the Thornes' butler."

Nancy was surprised.

"You can call me Wiggins. And you are . . .?"

Nancy told him.

"You see," Wiggins continued, "the estate lawyers hired me to look after the house. The assignment was only to last until a new buyer could be found, but when the new buyer turned up, he, too, wanted a butler. So I stayed on."

"I see. And Jessica—"

"Ah, yes, the thorny Miss Thorne. I hate her with a passion," Wiggins said mildly.

"You do? Why?"

"She's evil. Beyond hope. She gave her parents

nothing but trouble, and believe me, that lovely couple didn't deserve it."

"What did she do?"

Wiggins poured himself a glass of iced tea and sat down. He didn't slouch even when he was seated, she noticed. "You'd have better luck asking me what she didn't do. All-night parties, trouble with the law—you name it. She was out of control."

"That isn't the way she acts now. She acts like a perfect lady."

"Acting! Now, there's one thing she does do well. You should have seen her performance in court after she was arrested for stealing—"

"Stealing!"

"Shoplifting, actually. Can you imagine? With an allowance half as big as my salary she tried to nick a pair of blue jeans."

"That doesn't make sense. How come she's so wild?"

Wiggins sipped his tea. "I have a theory about that. I think she's bored. Some people crave a high level of excitement, you know. It's genetic. The Thornes' life-style was very quiet, so she got her kicks by being bad."

Nancy drummed her fingers on the tabletop and thought. The butler's theory made sense. In fact, Nancy had thought much the same thing about why Jessica had "fixed" her parachute.

"Was she arrested for anything else?" she asked.

"Oh, yes. Several things. That was before she left home for good. Later I lost track of her, though I heard rumors."

"What sort of rumors?"

"Well, there was talk of a scandal. It was hushed up, but supposedly she got involved with an older man. A politician. Married."

"Speaking of marriage, can you think of any reason she might want to get married now, to someone she doesn't love?"

"For thrills."

Nancy shook her head. "People don't marry for thrills. If they want thrills they stay single. I'm thinking of something like her parents' wills. Perhaps they set a condition—to receive her inheritance she has to be married."

It was Wiggins's turn to shake his head. "I can set you straight on that right now. The Thornes cut their daughter out of their wills entirely. They left everything to charity."

Nancy was stunned. So much for the inheritance theory! "What about relatives? Could someone else have set such a condition?"

"Jessica has no other living relatives."

"You're sure?"

"Absolutely. When her parents died, Jessica was left alone. She was also left quite penniless."

Then where had the thousand dollars in her hotel room come from? Nancy wondered to herself. She shifted uneasily. Then she rose to go.

"Thanks for the iced tea. And the information."

Wiggins walked her to the side door. As she was about to exit, Nancy turned.

"Oh, one more thing—does the name Scott O'Malley mean anything to you?"

The butler nodded gravely. "Indeed it does. Mr. O'Malley was the straw that broke the camel's back. He is the reason Mr. and Mrs. Thorne cut Jessica out of their wills."

"Who is he?"

"A welder by trade. A nice boy, actually, handsome, too. The Thornes disapproved of his family background, but his only real shortcoming was that he fell in love with Jessica."

"I don't understand," Nancy said. "What's wrong with that?"

"Oh, nothing. It's what Jessica did about it that rankled."

"I still don't get it. What did she do?"

Wiggins held himself straighter than ever. "My dear girl, she married him!"

Chapter

Ten

NANCY MANAGED TO limit her reaction to a lifted eyebrow. "Is she still married to him?"

He shrugged elegantly by lifting his square shoulders once.

"You don't know?"

"No, I'm afraid not."

"Okay, thanks again for your help. I won't take up any more of your time."

As quickly as she could without seeming rude, she walked down the driveway and leapt into her car.

* * *

Scott O'Malley's neighborhood was on the other side of Chicago, the South Side. The contrast between it and the Thornes' neighborhood was total. Jessica had grown up on a street full of mansions; Scott's street was lined with brick row houses. The yards here were tiny. The fences were chain link instead of wrought iron.

The address that Nancy had discovered in Jessica's hotel room corresponded to a house in the middle of the block. Its hedges were trimmed and its windows sparkled.

There was a tricycle in the middle of the front path. Stepping around it, Nancy went up to the door and rang the bell.

A young woman not much older than Nancy herself answered the door. She had short brown hair and wore a White Sox T-shirt.

"Yes?"

"Can you help me?" Nancy asked. "I'm trying to locate a Scott O'Malley."

The young woman frowned, then shook her head. "Sorry, never heard of him. You must have the wrong address."

"I don't think so. This address was given to me by a law firm in Billings, Montana."

"Are you from a collection agency?"

Nancy smiled reassuringly. "No, nothing like that."

"Sorry, I still can't help you. Wait a minute, I'll get my husband."

She disappeared. Nancy waited impatiently. She was certain about the address. She had the envelope with her. Perhaps the husband was Scott O'Malley with a new name.

A man in his early twenties came to the door. He was solidly built, had red hair that was longer than his wife's, and wore a Bears T-shirt. A sports-minded family, obviously.

"Scott O'Malley?"

"No, I'm Pat O'Gill."

"Excuse me—did you by any chance change your name from Scott O'Malley?"

"Nope. Pat's always been my name. Ask my mother," he said, grinning.

Nancy smiled back. "Can you tell me how to get in touch with Scott O'Malley? This is, or used to be, his address."

"Oh, I know who you want!" he said suddenly, snapping his fingers. "The former owners. Their name was O'Malley."

"A young couple? He's probably tall, dark-haired, square-jawed? She's thin, dark-haired, and very pretty?"

Pat O'Gill shook his head. "No, they were an older couple. Lived here twenty-five years, so I hear."

Must be Scott's parents, Nancy thought. "Do you know where I can find them now?"

"You can't. They're dead. We bought the house from the bank."

Nancy was disappointed. This wasn't going to be as easy as she had hoped.

"Maybe you could try our next-door neighbor." Pat pointed to a house on the left. "She probably knew the O'Malleys."

"Thanks."

"Good luck."

Nancy returned to the sidewalk, walked next door, and hurried up the front path. The house was almost identical to the O'Gills'. When she rang the bell a dog inside began to bark.

After a minute the door opened a crack. It was on a security chain. "What do you want?" a voice asked suspiciously.

"My name's Nancy Drew. I'm trying to locate a Scott O'Malley. The most recent address I have is next door, but—"

"O'Malley's dead. Died in a car crash with his wife."

"No, I'm looking for his son."

"Son's gone. Haven't seen him around in ages."

"Do you know where I can reach him?"

"No idea."

This was hopeless. Nancy turned to go. Then, on a sudden impulse, she turned back. "Does the name Jessica Thorne ring a bell?"

It was like saying "Open Sesame!" In seconds the security chain was off and the door was open wide. A thin, elderly woman wearing a dirty housedress gazed at her.

She had a large—very large—Doberman pinscher on a leash. "She's the one who should have died," the woman said tightly. "Not the O'Malleys. They were decent people."

"And Jessica wasn't?" Nancy asked quickly. She didn't want to lose her opening.

"That Jessica was bad news. A real uppity type. Thought she was God's gift. Well, she was pretty, all right, but I'm glad she's gone. Young Scott was a fool to marry her."

Nancy pressed on. "Are they still married?"

"Probably. Scott begged her for a divorce, but she wouldn't give him one. Never could understand that."

Nancy could hardly contain her excitement. This was the most promising news she had heard in days. She and Ned could use the information about the marriage as a wedge to make Jessica think they knew even more. Maybe then Jessica would tell them the rest.

"I have a few more questions about Jessica,"

Nancy said cautiously. "Do you mind if I come in?"

"No, I don't mind," the woman said. She held open the door.

That was easy, Nancy thought. A little too easy, really. The woman hadn't asked for identification—a careless lapse for someone who was obviously worried about being robbed.

Walking into the woman's living room was like walking back in time. The pink and turquoise over-stuffed chairs, the kidney-shaped coffee table, and the huge TV with the small screen were all the latest fashion—circa 1955.

The woman pointed toward the sofa, then flopped into an armchair. "Have a seat. I'm Margaret Ryan." The dog lay down at her feet.

Nancy sat. "You seem to have known Jessica well, Ms. Ryan," she prompted. "How long did she live next door?"

"Too long. About a year, I guess. Stayed there even after she drove her husband off. That's the kind of mooch she was."

"She drove her husband off?"

"Certainly. She was always after him to buy her things. Perfume, clothes, even an airplane! Imagine that? Around here, people are lucky if they have a car. Anyway, no man could put up with that for long. So he took off."

"Where did he go—do you have any idea?"

"Nope. Left without a word. Just about broke his parents' hearts. They never heard from him again before they died."

"So Scott and Jessica were living with Mr. and Mrs. O'Malley?"

"Yup, had a bedroom in the basement. But that wasn't enough for Miss Priss." Margaret Ryan's mouth twisted in disgust. "Oh, no. After Scott left she put the O'Malleys in the basement and took the second story for herself."

Nancy was shocked. "They let her get away with that?"

"More the fools. They felt guilty about Scott walking out on her."

"How long ago did Scott take off?"

"About six months ago, I guess."

"When were the O'Malleys killed?"

"Two months ago. That's definite."

Nancy leaned back and digested that. A clearer picture of Jessica's game was beginning to form in her mind. But she had quite a few more questions.

Leaning forward again she asked, "Earlier you called Jessica a mooch. Why? Did she take money from the O'Malleys?"

"T-Take—take money!" the woman sputtered. "Why, she practically stripped them of their life savings, that shameless—"

"She played on their guilt, I'm sure," Nancy said. "It sounds like there wasn't much left when they were killed."

"No, and what there was that hussy took, too," she spat. "She stayed on about a month, then one day she up and sold their house."

That was about the time that she had appeared in River Heights, Nancy realized. It also explained where she got her cash.

"Jessica's a real operator, all right," Nancy confirmed. "Tell me something else. Why wouldn't she divorce Scott?"

"Like I said, I never did understand that. He begged for six months, almost from the day they were married. She kept saying no."

"So he took off."

"That's right. Didn't seem to bother her any though. She kept doing exactly what she was doing: going out with her rich friends, spending money, acting like a snob. Why she bothered living next door I can't imagine."

Nancy could. She had needed the O'Malleys' money. Her parents had left her penniless. Jessica was a mooch, all right.

"One more question, Ms. Ryan. Are you sure the O'Malleys died in a car crash?"

"Positive," the woman confirmed. "Jessica didn't kill them, if that's what you're wondering."

That was exactly what Nancy had been wondering. The death of two sets of parents so close together was a long coincidence, but it seemed to be exactly that—a coincidence.

Nancy rose. "Thank you, Ms. Ryan, you've been very helpful."

The old woman, who had been so hostile at first, was now reluctant to let Nancy go. "Would you like something to drink, dear?"

"No, thanks. I have to run."

A few minutes later she was on her way back to River Heights.

"How'd it go in Chicago?" Ned asked her over the phone.

Nancy was in her room, pacing back and forth. The cord on her telephone was stretched to its limit.

"I learned a lot, and none of it's good," she announced.

"What's the story?"

Nancy gave him the details. "Jessica's been keeping O'Malley secret," she said. "When she realizes that we know all about him she may tell us more."

Nancy expected to hear something, but there was only silence on the other end of the line.

"Ned, aren't you going to say anything?" she asked.

"It won't work," Ned pronounced.

Nancy's mouth fell open. "Why not? I admit we'll have to handle it carefully . . ."

Ned's voice was heavy with disappointment. "I'm sorry, Nancy, but we're out of luck. Jessica carefully . . ."told me all about her marriage to Scott O'Malley today."

"Oh, no!"

"Oh, yes. And wait, it gets worse. Not only did she admit that she was married, she also told me something else—"

"I think I know what you're about to say."

"You guessed it. Jessica is divorced!"

Chapter

Eleven

NANCY WAS STUNNED. How did Jessica always manage to stay one step ahead of them?

She rubbed her temple. "Okay, let me get this straight. Jessica *says* that she got a divorce from Scott O'Malley."

"Right."

"But she can't prove it."

"Oh, she says she can. She made a point of mentioning that."

"You didn't ask her? She brought it up herself?"

"Uh-huh."

"She could be bluffing."

"It's possible."

Maybe things weren't as bad as they looked. Nancy thought it over, then switched the receiver to her other ear.

"According to Margaret Ryan, Jessica refused to give O'Malley a divorce," she said.

"That's strange," Ned said. "I wonder why?"

"Maybe she wanted to continue sponging off him and his family."

"Maybe. But if that's true, wouldn't she have granted him a divorce after his parents died and the money ran out?"

"Sure, if she could find him! He disappeared, remember?"

"True." Ned paused. "Hold on, couldn't she get a divorce anyway?"

"Without his consent? Yes, under Illinois law she could. But not this soon. It would take six to eight months to get the decree."

"Nancy, how do you know all this stuff about divorce?" Ned asked in surprise.

"You forget, my dad's a lawyer."

"Oh, yeah."

Trailing the telephone cord behind her, Nancy went to her bed and flopped onto her back. She was starting to feel optimistic again.

"Okay, so here's what we've got—Jessica says she's divorced, but the evidence says otherwise. She must be lying."

"We can't prove that," Ned stated.

"*We* can't. But there's someone who can. Scott O'Malley."

"If we can find him."

"I'll go to work on it first thing tomorrow."

She and Ned discussed how to track Scott down. When she was satisfied with the plan, she asked, "What's new on your end?"

"Not much," Ned said. "Wait a minute, there is one strange thing. I went back to the jeweler's in the mall, the one where Jessica and I ordered our wedding rings. Remember?"

"How could I forget!"

"I wanted to see if the rings had arrived. They had, but Jessica had stopped by already to pick them up."

"So?"

"Here's the thing: She only took one—mine!"

"Maybe she wants you to pick up hers. It would make sense. In a wedding ceremony the rings are *exchanged.*"

"No, you don't understand," Ned pressed. "She told the jeweler that we only needed one, for me. She told him to return the other one."

Nancy sat up. "That is weird."

Another puzzle. Nancy wrestled with the new clue for a while, but couldn't make sense of it. Never mind, she thought. One thing at a time. Find Scott O'Malley.

A few minutes later she said good night to Ned and went to sleep.

The next morning, Nancy went to her father's study armed with a legal pad and pencil. Sitting at his desk, she dialed a number.

"Good morning, Mr. Pike. It's Nancy Drew. Had any luck tracing those clippings?"

"'Morning, Nancy. Yes, I've tracked them all down. I've also got the names of all the boys in the photos for you."

"Fantastic! How did you do it?"

"Easy. I phoned the sports editors of each paper, gave them dates and descriptions of the photos, and asked them to supply the missing captions. They all came through."

Nancy snatched up her pencil. "Okay, I'm ready. Let me have them."

Mr. Pike read a list of names and towns. A few phone numbers were supplied, too, but Nancy realized that she would have to get most of them from Directory Information.

"Terrific, Mr. Pike," she said when he had finished. "How can I thank you?"

"The usual way," he said.

"It's a deal. The *Record* gets an exclusive when I crack my next case."

Mr. Pike chuckled. "Looking forward to it."

Nancy hung up and went to work. It took most of the morning to contact all the boys on the list, but finally she did. The results were disappointing. Not one of them had ever heard of Jessica Thorne or Scott O'Malley.

The clippings had led her down a blind alley.

After lunch she returned to the phone. Tracing Scott O'Malley proved a little easier. Pretending to be a secretary in the accounting department of a fictitious company, she called the River Heights office of the welders' union. She had an overtime check for Scott O'Malley, she told them, but he had moved away from the address in her records. Could they locate him?

They could. Within an hour the union's national headquarters phoned her with his current address. He was living in Gary, Indiana. It was too late to fly there that day, so she decided to get a good night's sleep and go in the morning.

The city of Gary looked desperate. It was an old steel-mill town suffering from the collapse of the steel industry. Buildings were boarded up, and the stores that had not fled to the suburbs were not doing much business.

At last she found Scott O'Malley's street. It wasn't nearly so nice as his street on Chicago's South Side. Litter was strewn about, and several buildings were obviously abandoned.

Scott himself lived in a rickety wooden apartment building. There were no interior halls, just outside stairways and landings. She walked up to the third floor—and listened. A radio was blaring music in his apartment.

She knocked on the door. The volume of the music went down. A moment later the door opened. The young man who stood before her bore a mild resemblance to Ned: muscular build, dark hair, square jaw. He also had the same devastating soft, dark eyes. Nancy rated him a hunk and a half to Ned's two.

"Scott O'Malley?"

"Yes?"

"My name's Nancy Drew."

"Uh—are you from a collection agency?" he asked nervously.

That made twice recently that she had been asked that question!

"No, I'm a private detective, and—"

He bolted. Shoving her out of the way, he charged down the stairs.

Nancy followed. Now that she had found him she wasn't about to let him go until she got the answers she needed.

117

He was fast, she had to give him that. Even in bare feet he nearly outdistanced her. But Nancy was an excellent sprinter. She managed to stay an even thirty yards behind him.

He turned down an alley, leapt over a fence and zipped across a weed-strewn yard. Nancy followed. He leapt the fence on the far side, but then she heard a cry of pain.

He had cut his foot on a shard of glass. Climbing over the fence, Nancy offered him a handkerchief from her purse.

"You need to clean that cut and get a bandage on it," she said.

Scott pressed the handkerchief to the wound. "I'm not giving her another penny!" he shouted. "Can't you see I'm broke?"

"Her? Who are you talking about?" Nancy asked, though she suspected she knew.

"Jessica. That's who you're working for, isn't it?"

"As a matter of fact, no."

Scott looked surprised. "You're not?"

"No, I represent someone else. I just want to ask you a few questions. This won't get back to Jessica, I promise."

Scott looked distrustful. Nevertheless, he agreed to help her. They went back to his apartment. When he had washed and bandaged the cut they sat down at his kitchen table.

"Okay, first question," Nancy began. "Are you and Jessica divorced?"

"No. I tried to get a divorce, but she contested it. My lawyer said she could keep me tied up in court for years."

Nancy's heart leapt. "Why did she fight you?"

"I don't know."

"There must be a reason."

Scott nodded. "Yeah, I've thought about it a lot since I ran away. It's probably got something to do with money. That's pretty much all Jessica ever wanted from me."

"I don't quite understand," Nancy said. "Welding pays all right, but not a fortune. And your parents weren't rich."

"You're right. I think it was my aunt's money she was after."

"Your *aunt's* money?"

"Her name is Kathleen O'Malley. She married a rancher out west and inherited a five-thousand-acre ranch when he died. She's loaded."

"And the property will come to you when she dies?"

Scott rubbed his forearm. "That's right. Don't get me wrong, I love Aunt Kathleen a lot. I hope she lives a good long time."

"This ranch—is it in Montana, by any chance?" Nancy asked.

"How did you know that? It's near Billings."

Nancy nodded. Some large pieces of the puzzle were falling into place. "Scott, I hate to ask you this, but have you been in touch with your aunt Kathleen lately?"

He rubbed his right forearm some more. "Not lately. Last time I saw her was at my parents' wake. I didn't get to talk to her much though. Jessica was hounding me, so I cut out fast."

Nancy swallowed. "Scott, I have to break some bad news—I think your aunt is dead."

"What!" Scott turned pale. "Are you sure about that?"

Nancy pulled out the envelope that she had taken from Jessica's hotel room. "Pretty sure. This arrived at your Chicago address about a month ago. It's from a Billings law firm, and I think they were informing you of her death."

Scott took the envelope with trembling fingers and opened it. "Hold on, there's no letter inside."

"No, Jessica has it," Nancy told him. "That's why I can't be sure of what it said."

"How did you get the envelope, then?" he asked. Dropping it on the table top, he went back to rubbing his arm.

"I'd rather not say," Nancy hedged. "Uh, Scott—do you mind if I ask you something?"

"You've asked me plenty already. Shoot."

"Why do you keep rubbing your arm?"

He grimaced. "Oh, that. Well, I fractured it about a year ago. It still feels sore from time to time."

Nancy sat bolt upright. A thousand alarm bells went off in her head. A broken arm! That was the connection! Of course! She didn't yet have Jessica's whole plan worked out—that would take more time—but at least now she knew why Jessica had zeroed in on Ned.

She leapt up. "Scott, we've got to fly to River Heights right away."

"River Heights?" he asked. "Why do I have to go there?"

"You've got to tell your story to the police," she explained. "I haven't got it all worked out just yet, but if my theory is correct your wife is planning to murder my boyfriend!"

Chapter

Twelve

BEFORE THEY LEFT, Nancy made two calls. The first was to the law firm in Billings, Montana. It confirmed what she had already guessed: Scott's aunt was dead. Furthermore, she had left her entire estate to Scott—or to his wife, provided that he, too, was dead.

She conveyed the news to Scott with heartfelt sympathy, then—after pausing a minute to consider what Jessica was likely to do next—she dialed a second number on his phone.

"Mrs. Nickerson?"

"Hello, Nancy," Ned's mother said. "You sound like you're calling long distance."

"I am. Is Ned there?"

"No, he's at work, but I expect him home for dinner."

"Oh, thank goodness." Relieved, Nancy put her hand on her chest. "I was afraid that—oh, never mind. Will you please do me a favor?"

"Anything. Just name it."

"Keep Ned away from Jessica. He's in terrible danger."

"Oh, no!"

"I'm afraid it's true. Be especially sure he doesn't get on an airplane with her, okay? This is life or death."

"Nancy, you're scaring me! What's going on?"

"Mrs. Nickerson, I haven't got it completely worked out, but for now there's one thing you should know: Ned never intended to marry Jessica. It was only a sham."

There was a shocked silence, then, "Well, that's a relief! But why?"

"We've been investigating her. Tell Ned I've made a breakthrough."

"Can you tell me about it?"

"It would take too long. When you see Ned, just tell him that Jessica's motive is definitely money. There's an inheritance involved, a look-alike husband, a broken arm—"

"Wait! I'm writing this down," Mrs. Nickerson interrupted. There was a pause while she scribbled some notes. "Money—inheritance—look-alike—broken arm. My goodness, this is very mysterious. What does it mean?"

"I'll explain when I get back to River Heights," Nancy promised. "I need time to put it all together. But don't worry, if you keep Ned at home he'll be safe."

"I'll keep him here," his mother promised. "You can count on it. I'll even lock him in his room, if necessary."

Nancy smiled. "Thanks, Mrs. Nickerson. See you in a few hours."

At the Gary airport a short while later, Nancy taxied her rented Cessna to the top of a runway. Scott was in the passenger seat. He was shaken by the news of his aunt's death, but he took it stoically. He was eager to help Nancy out, and to learn just what Jessica was up to.

Nancy quickly ran through a pretakeoff check. The instruments and electrical systems checked out, as did the controls. She radioed the tower for clearance, then taxied onto the runway centerline, facing into the wind.

She pushed the throttle into the wide open position and waited. The plane began to roll. Taking off was easy; all she had to do was get to 60 mph and the plane did the rest.

When they reached cruising altitude and speed, she relaxed.

"Can you tell me what's going on now?" Scott asked. "Who's your boyfriend and why is Jessica going to murder him?"

Nancy thought for a few minutes before she answered. Not until she was certain that she had Jessica's plan fully worked out did she finally fill Scott in.

"His name's Ned Nickerson, and she's planning to murder him because she needs a dead body. Not just any dead body will do, either. It has to be square-jawed and a certain height and weight. It's also got to have a right arm with bones that've been broken and healed."

"Like mine."

"Exactly. You see, she needs money. Lots of it. She's got a taste for high living, and her parents cut her out of their wills."

"Don't I know it!" Scott groaned. "She nearly drove me crazy with all her demands. 'Buy me this, buy me that . . .'"

"Must've been horrible," she sympathized. "But count yourself lucky. If you hadn't run away, yours is the body she would have used."

"Are you serious?"

"Perfectly. She knew you were due to inherit a fortune from your aunt, and I think she wants it all for herself."

Scott nodded. "That fits. She's the greediest person I've ever known. Sometimes I can't believe I married her."

"Well, she's beautiful. And smart. She knows how to get what she wants."

"Amen! But how did she pick out your boyfriend? You're not from Chicago."

"When Jessica got that letter from the law firm, she cooked up a plan and started looking through old issues of newspapers in the library. She checked the photos in the sports pages for boys of your height, weight, and general appearance—"

"Why the sports pages?"

Nancy shook her head in admiration. "Because athletes are more likely to have broken their arms. Anyway, she cut out pictures and made some calls, but no luck. Then she came across Ned's picture. Bingo! It ran with a story about him breaking his arm. She drew X's through all the other pictures and stuffed them in an envelope—"

"The one from the law firm?"

"Right. Then she sold your parents' house, packed her bags, traveled to River Heights, tracked down Ned, and got 'lost' while jogging in his neighborhood."

"That's how she met him?"

"Yes." Nancy explained how the phony engagement had come about.

"That's Jessica all right," Scott said when she had finished. "When she wants to, she can be persuasive as all get-out. But tell me, what good would killing your boyfriend do? He's not me. One look at his body would prove that."

"Ah, that's just it! It's *how* she's going to kill him that makes the difference."

"What do you mean?"

"Here's her plan. She's going to take Ned up in a small plane. Fly him far away. Then she'll drug him—she's got a full bottle of sleeping pills in her hotel room for just that purpose—then she'll bail out. It'll be easy. She's got her pilot's license, and she knows how to skydive."

"I still don't get it."

"Don't you see? Without a pilot the plane will crash and burn. Ned's body will be charred beyond recognition. She'll say he's you, and the coroner will confirm it from height, weight, and skeletal evidence, like the broken arm."

"Really? That's all a coroner needs to make an ID?"

"No. Here's where she gets really clever. The best method of identifying corpses is through dental records. Now, I think she stole Ned's X-rays from his dentist's office. If so, she'll put your name on them and show them to the coroner. Bingo! Scott O'Malley will be officially dead."

"What happens if I decide to go visit my aunt someday?" Scott wanted to know. "If I show up, Jessica's plan is finished."

Nancy shook her head. "Don't be so sure. She's already proved she's cold-blooded enough to kill. Scott, I hate to say it, but if you got in Jessica's way I'm sure she wouldn't hesitate to murder you, too."

"And keep my inheritance all to herself." Scott shuddered.

"That's right. Diabolical, huh?"

"I'll say," he agreed. "Good old Jess has been busy."

Nancy had to agree. Busy and smart. Too bad *she* hadn't been as clever. If she had, she would have cracked the case long before. Lots of clues had been staring her in the face all along—like the missing dental X-rays. She was almost positive Jessica had stolen them.

They flew along in silence for a while. Nancy consulted her chart and made several course changes. There was a slight crosswind, and it was blowing them sideways.

When she was five minutes from the River Heights airport, Nancy made radio contact. She was cleared to land.

"You must be a pretty good detective to have figured all that out," Scott said, breaking the silence.

"Pretty good. I wish I'd done better. For one thing, I let Jessica's acting confuse me. In the beginning, I was pretty sure she was after money, but when she turned down a car that my boyfriend offered to buy her, I rejected that as a motive."

"Jessica turned down a car?"

"On the grounds that they had to save money."

"Jessica save money? That's a laugh," Scott said bitterly.

"Yeah, some joke," Nancy agreed. "You know what else I missed? The money she *was* after. Since Ned isn't rich, and since there was no major inheritance due to either of them, I assumed that no bequest was involved."

"But there was a bequest. It came from *my* family, that's all," Scott supplied.

"I wish I had guessed that. I gave up my inheritance theory too easily."

"Don't blame yourself. You didn't even know I existed," Scott consoled her. "Anyway, it's all going to turn out all right."

"Yes, thank goodness I found you before she executed her plan—and Ned!"

A short while later they reached the airport.

Nancy circled while another small plane took off, then glided down to the runway. Ten minutes later they were inside the main terminal.

Nancy phoned the Nickersons' house. "Mrs. Nickerson? It's Nancy. I'll be right over. Is everything okay?"

Mrs. Nickerson's voice was trembling with fear. "Oh, Nancy, it's awful. I tried to do what you told me, but—but—" She stopped and broke into anguished sobs.

"Mrs. Nickerson, calm down! What's wrong? Tell me what happened!"

Ned's father came onto the line. "Nancy, Jessica and Ned are gone!"

Chapter

Thirteen

OH, NO! How did it happen?"

Mr. Nickerson explained grimly. "I had just arrived home from work when Ned came in. Unfortunately, Edith was outside in the garden and didn't see Ned arrive. She hadn't yet told me about your call. Ned said he was flying to Detroit with Jessica—"

"Flying!"

"Yes, to see some relatives of hers. Well, naturally I didn't think anything about it. I said I'd see him later."

"Mr. Nickerson, Jessica doesn't have any relatives. Not in Detroit, or anywhere else," she said.

"So what's going on? What is this trip all about?"

Nancy told him. There was no longer any reason to hold back.

Mr. Nickerson's rage was fearsome. "She's going to pay for this! I don't care if it takes the rest of my life . . . I'm going to make sure she lands in jail! I'm also angry at you and Ned, Nancy. How could you have gotten involved in such a dangerous scheme without telling us?"

"But we didn't think it was dangerous when we started out," she explained. "Anyway, right now the important thing is to stop them. I'm going right to work on it. I'll keep you informed."

Hanging up, Nancy dashed to the F.A.A. office near the control tower, where she explained the situation and asked if Jessica could be grounded. The officer on duty shook his head.

"If she touches down we can see that she doesn't get permission to take off again. But she's already in the air, right?"

"I think so," Nancy said, remembering the plane that was taking off as she was landing.

"Then it's going to be tough to stop her. Let's see if she filed a flight plan."

They checked the records. Jessica had indeed filed a plan. It showed the registration number of her rented plane and her destination: Detroit. But Nancy didn't buy it.

"She's not headed for Detroit, I'll bet anything on it."

"Where's she going, then?"

"Montana, probably. Crashing the plane there will shorten the time and paperwork involved in claiming the inheritance."

"Makes sense," said Scott, who was with her.

Nancy made a decision. "I'm going after her. The only way to stop her may be to catch her en route. Do you have a chart handy?"

"Right here," the F.A.A. officer said. He pulled it out.

Nancy opened it and quickly drew a pencil line from River Heights to Billings, Montana. Then she made a list of small airports along the way and handed it to the officer.

"Can you phone ahead to these airports? Ask them to be on the lookout. If Jessica makes radio contact, or if she touches down for any reason, they should stop her."

"I'll see what I can do."

"Thanks. I'm going to rerent my plane. Let's go, Scott."

As it turned out, it was another twenty minutes before Nancy was ready to go. First, Mr. Nickerson arrived at the airport. Bess and George were close behind him.

"We'd dropped by Ned's house to see him," Bess explained. "Mr. Nickerson told us the whole story, so we drove out here."

Nancy thought. "Can you guys go with me? I could use some extra pairs of eyes."

"You got it." George nodded.

"Count me in too," Bess said. "I want to be there when Jessica gets arrested."

Nancy nodded. "Don't we all! Will you guys go buy some sandwiches and soda? It's going to be dinnertime soon, and I think we'll be in the air for quite a while."

"No sooner said than done," George promised. She and Bess departed.

Mr. Nickerson cleared his throat. "While you're chasing them I'm going to phone the FBI. We need their help."

"Let's hope we get it," Scott said. "We should, since she'll be going across state lines."

Nancy smiled. She felt better knowing that she had so much backup support. Wasting no more time, she went back to the rental office. Luckily, they had a larger, faster plane to give her. It was faster than Jessica's plane too.

A short while later Nancy, Scott, Bess, and George were in the air. Nancy banked the plane until she was on course for Billings, Montana. Then she brought her friends up to date.

When she was finished, Bess whistled in

amazement. "How cold-blooded!" she commented over the all-out roar of the engine.

"I can't believe Jessica! Imagine spending all that time with Ned, knowing that she was going to kill him," George added.

Nancy thought about it. "It's weird, but not that unusual. Sometimes killers are very close to their victims."

"That's true," George said.

"Keep in mind something else—Jessica's not planning to kill him with her own hands," Nancy added. "The plane crash will take care of Ned."

Bess spoke up again. She was in the passenger seat directly behind Nancy. "There's something I don't understand. How will Jessica explain that *she* bailed out but Ned didn't?"

"She'll make up a story. She'll say something like, she begged him to jump, too, but Ned insisted on trying to save the plane," Nancy guessed.

"Sounds logical."

"I've got another question," George said. "How will she get Ned to take the sleeping pills?"

"She won't. I assume she'll dissolve a bunch of them in a cup of coffee or something and give *that* to him," Nancy replied. "That's the obvious way."

They flew without speaking for a while. Nancy scanned the sky ahead through a pair of binoculars. It was futile, though, she knew. It would be three hours or more before they caught Jessica—that was, *if* she was right and Ned's would-be murderer was heading for Montana.

She didn't let herself think about the possibility that she was wrong. Onward she flew, flying slightly north and west from Chicago.

They ate their sandwiches in grim silence. "Where do you think she'll try to crash the plane?" Bess asked, breaking the silence.

"Right over the Montana border," Nancy said.

George consulted the chart. "Won't it be dark out by the time she gets there?"

"Not quite," Nancy said. "Remember that we're going east to west, crossing a time zone. We're flying into the sun, so it will still be light."

She hoped they would catch Jessica well before then however. As they passed airports, Nancy called them on the radio. Most were expecting her call, but none had news to report. Jessica had neither hailed them nor landed.

Nancy grew worried. What if she was wrong? What if Jessica was heading off in a completely different direction?

As they crossed the Iowa border, Scott spoke up. "I really feel terrible about this."

"It isn't your fault," Nancy said kindly.

"I suppose not, but I still feel bad," Scott said.

"Anyway, at least I've learned something from this experience—"

"What's that?" George asked.

"Teenagers should think twice before getting married!"

They all laughed. It was nervous laughter though. The tension in the cramped cockpit did not diminish.

On the ground below, miles and miles of perfectly square fields went by. The land looked like a chessboard, but who was winning the game, Nancy wondered? She or Jessica?

The sun sank lower in the sky. Although they were making good time, they might run out of daylight, Nancy knew.

Then, just north of Sioux City, they got lucky. Nancy radioed a small airfield and heard the news she had been waiting for.

"A plane with that registration number just left here," the control tower said.

Nancy said a silent prayer of thanks. "Couldn't you stop them?"

"Didn't know we were supposed to," the tower replied. "We just got a call from the FBI a couple of minutes ago."

"Never mind. How long ago did the plane take off?"

"Five, six minutes."

"All right! Thank you! Over and out."

She wanted to shout for joy. They were just ahead!

The throttle was already all the way out. It was impossible to gain more airspeed. Nancy balanced the controls so she could keep her hands free, then peered through the binoculars.

Ten minutes later she spotted them. They were half a mile to her left and one hundred feet lower in altitude.

"I see them! I can read the registration number on their fuselage!"

Cheers broke out.

Suddenly Nancy's stomach plunged. As she watched, a tiny figure wearing a parachute fell away from the plane.

Jessica! They were too late! She was plummeting toward the ground. In a minute or less the plane would crash—with Ned inside!

Chapter

Fourteen

NANCY RACKED HER brains for a way to save Ned. Desperately, she jerked the radio's microphone from its holder and jabbed the button.

"This is Nancy Drew calling Ned Nickerson! Nancy Drew calling Ned Nickerson! Ned, is the radio on? Can you read me?"

No response.

She tried again, her voice rising in panic. "Ned, come in! Ned, come in—oh, please! If you can hear me, wake up! This is an emergency! You have to take the wheel!"

Nothing.

Quickly she explained the situation to the others. "Hurry, I need ideas!"

But no one could think of anything to do. It seemed that Ned was doomed. Drugged and unconscious, he would be unable to fly the plane. It was still flying steadily, but sooner or later it would stall and dive.

Nancy was frantic. In desperation she tried the radio one more time. "Ned, if you can hear me, please try—*try* to wake up! Oh, please, Ned— please, please answer me!"

Nothing.

In a flash, the realization dawned upon her: Ned was going to die. There was nothing she could do to prevent it. There was no way to reach him, no way to get to the plane herself and take the controls. She had lost.

The next moment she was filled with resolve. Jessica was *not* going to get away! No matter what, she had to be brought to justice. Seizing the wheel, Nancy banked hard to the left. In no time they were going back the way they had come.

"Nancy, what are you doing! Why are you turning around?" Bess gasped.

"We're going after Jessica."

"But what about Ned?"

"I can't think of a way to save him. Can you?"

Gloomy silence filled the cabin. Grief was thick in the air.

Grabbing the binoculars again, Nancy looked for Jessica. There! Her chute was open. She was drifting down toward a field that was near a suburban housing development. Nancy could see a tiny column of smoke rising from a barbecue.

George, who was sitting in the forward passenger seat, spotted Jessica's chute at the same time that Nancy did. She checked the altimeter. "Nancy, we're two thousand feet off the ground! How are we going to catch her?"

Her friend had a point. Jessica would reach the ground long before they could land. She might get away.

Unless . . .

Suddenly, Nancy cut back the throttle. At the same time she pressed the left rudder pedal hard. The plane began to turn and lose altitude. Normally, she would have pulled back the wheel to ease the descent, but this time she didn't. They continued down in a rapid spiral.

"Nancy, what are you doing!" Bess screamed. "I think I'm going to throw up!"

"Hang on! We're taking the quick way down!"

Anxiously, she kept her eye on the altimeter. Its large hand swirled around the dial dangerously fast.

At last, just two hundred feet off the ground, she stopped the turn and flew level. Ahead was the field where Jessica was going to land. She studied it. It was empty but rutted with furrows. Too rough for a landing.

Then she spotted a level, unpaved trail down the middle. That would be the trail used by trucks during harvest. She could land there. Upping the throttle slightly, she headed for it. Ahead, Jessica hit the ground.

"Hold on, we're going in for a landing!" she warned the others.

The plane sank, heading for its landing. Nancy dropped the flaps. She knew it would have to be perfect. A few feet off the ground she raised the nose, and the plane settled to the ground. Immediately it began to bounce and lurch. The dusty trail was not built for planes to land.

A hundred yards to the right, Jessica collapsed her chute and began to undo her harness. She glanced at the plane.

When they were coasting slowly, Nancy applied the brakes and cut the engine. In a flash she undid her seat belt and snapped open her door. She leapt out and ran.

Jessica recognized the flash of Nancy's red-gold hair instantly. She began to run. Fear gave her extra speed, and Nancy saw that she was pulling away. She might escape!

But Jessica hadn't counted on Scott. In a burst of speed, her husband sprinted past Nancy. Running like a madman, her burned up the distance between them in seconds.

"Gotcha!" he roared as he tackled her. Jessica went down like a rag doll.

When Nancy caught up to them, Jessica was cursing. Scott twisted her right arm behind her back. "Let me go!" she screamed.

"No chance, Jess," he said. "And don't bother thinking up any stories. We know exactly what you're up to."

Nancy stopped running. Her shoulders slumped. It was over. They had Jessica, but what about Ned? Sadly, she shaded her eyes and scanned the horizon. Somewhere ahead there would be a column of thick, black smoke. It would mark the spot where his plane had crashed. But Nancy couldn't see any smoke.

Then she heard it. . . .

It was a low rumble at first, barely audible. It grew louder. George and Bess ran up full of questions. Nancy waved them silent. "Hear that?" she asked. "It's a plane!"

The next second it burst into sight over a clump of trees to one side of the field. It was

Jessica's plane! Nancy could read the registration number clearly.

It zoomed overhead, not fifty feet off the ground. As it did, the plane's wings wiggled back and forth in a friendly greeting. Nancy knew instantly what that meant.

Ned was safe!

Chapter

Fifteen

NED LANDED HIS plane just behind Nancy's. The second he stepped out Nancy leapt into his arms.

"Oh, Ned, I can't believe it! You're safe. You're safe!" she cried.

"Not even a hair out of place," he joked.

"But how? The sleeping pills—didn't she slip some into your—"

"Coffee? Yes, she did. But I didn't drink it. I poured it out," he explained. "You see, I read some notes that my mom had scribbled on a pad by the phone. Your name was at the top. The notes didn't give me the whole story, but they gave me enough. Thanks to you, I was able to figure out Jessica's plan."

"Wait a minute! If you figured it out, then why did you get in the plane? Didn't you realize she wanted to kill you?"

"Well, not right away. It took a while to piece it all together. Here's what happened: Thanks to my mom's notes I was on my guard. At the airport I pretended to go to the men's room, but really I only went around a corner. I watched Jessica buy a cup of coffee from a vending machine. When I got back she handed it to me."

"You saw her doctor it?"

"Not exactly, but I suspected that something was up. I went outside and poured the coffee into the grass. Sure enough, in the bottom of the cup were a bunch of half-dissolved capsules!"

"What happened then?"

Ned stretched his muscles. "About ten minutes into the flight I started yawning. Finally I slumped and pretended to be unconscious. Jessica pinched me to make sure I was out. It hurt, but somehow I managed not to flinch."

"Oh, Ned!" Nancy was appalled. "That flight lasted hours! Did you really go all that time without moving?"

"Yes, that was the bad part," he confirmed.

"The good part was that I had plenty of time to think. That's when everything started to make sense . . . the look-alike, the broken arm—all of it. I guessed she was planning to kill me. The only question was when would she jump out of the plane. Now, tell me, how did *you* work it out?"

Rapidly, Nancy told him about finding Scott O'Malley and about the fortune he was due to inherit from his aunt.

By this time Bess and George had joined them. Scott came up, too, dragging the dusty and unwilling Jessica with him. Ned repeated his story from the beginning.

Jessica turned to her husband angrily. "This is all your fault!" she hissed. "If you hadn't run away, I wouldn't have had to go find someone who could double as you!"

Scott shook his head in amazement. To Nancy, it looked as if he was seeing, for the first time, how ugly his wife really was.

"Jess, don't give me that. No one made you hatch a murder plot."

"That's right, you did it all on your own!" Bess stated. Her courage had come back now that they were safely on the ground.

George scuffed the dust with her toe. "I hate to say this, but there's still something I don't get.

Why didn't she just track down Scott and murder *him*, instead of going through this elaborate plan to kill Ned? Sorry, Scott."

"That's okay," he assured her. "It's a natural question."

"And I think I can answer it," Nancy said. "I'll bet she tried, but she couldn't locate him. She didn't think of tracing him through the welders' union, as I did. Do I have that right, Jessica?"

Jessica didn't reply. Instead she snarled and lunged for Nancy. Scott held her back. She cried out as he twisted her wrist.

Nancy shook her head. "There're a couple of things *I* don't understand. Why didn't you answer me on the radio, Ned?"

"I didn't hear anything. Maybe when Jessica slammed her fist against the radio some wires came loose."

"Why did she jump out here in Iowa instead of in Montana?"

"I can tell you that," Ned put in. "You see, she was monitoring the radio and she heard you call that little airport where we stopped for fuel. After that she panicked. That was when she bashed the radio. She bailed out, even though there was no longer any chance that she could carry out the rest of her plan."

"Bad move. Bailing out changes this crime

from intent to commit murder to *attempted* murder," Nancy said.

Once again, Jessica strained to get away from Scott. "Nickerson, you should be dead!" she spat. "How did you land that plane?"

Nancy answered for him. "Jessica, didn't you know?" she asked sweetly. "Ned has his pilot's license too!"

After that, Jessica said no more. Several residents from the nearby development walked up to see what was going on. Nancy asked if she could use a phone, and soon she had contacted the local police and the FBI.

A short while later Jessica was taken away. She would be held in the local jail until the following morning. Back at the field, Nancy locked up the planes for the night. Then she and Ned walked hand in hand toward a nearby house. A local resident had offered to put everyone from River Heights up for the night.

Suddenly Nancy stopped. Lifting Ned's hand with her own, she said, "Wait a minute—what's that on your finger?"

Ned unlaced his fingers and glanced down. "Oh—my wedding ring. Jessica slipped it on before she jumped."

"So that's why she took your ring from the jewelers! It was true: She only needed one! It was more evidence to prove that you were really Scott O'Malley."

"Yup," Ned confirmed. He pulled off the ring. "You know something, Nancy? I don't want to think about marriage again for a long time."

"I agree. I've had enough of this marriage stuff myself."

"When we get back home, what do you say we go on a nice, normal date," Ned suggested.

Nancy smiled. "You're on. No proposals?"

"No proposals. Oh, except maybe one—"

"What?"

Taking both her hands in his, Ned gazed deeply into her eyes. "Nancy, will you do me the honor of—giving me a kiss?"

Laughing, Nancy pulled her hands away and shoved him. "You nut!"

"No kiss?" he asked, crestfallen.

"Well—"

And that was the last thing she said for a long time.

Nancy's next case:

Nancy and Carson Drew are in New York for a rare vacation together. Nancy needs a break, and her father has promised her Broadway shows, candlelight dinners, and a shopping spree. But no sooner do they check into the Plaza Hotel than Nancy becomes curious about wealthy Sarah Amberly and her family, who have the suite next door.

One day, when her father's off on business, Nancy hears strange sounds coming from the suite. She finds Sarah Amberly collapsed, clutching her heart. Strange how none of her loving family were around to give her her heart medicine. Could one of them be out to get Sarah's money? It's starting to look like a family affair . . . in *RICH AND DANGEROUS*, Case #25 in The Nancy Drew Files™.

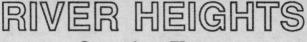